Praise for Th  bles

"Herein lie great words and lines of wit and wisdom as might be read by a father to a son, or, for that matter, a mother to a father while a daughter stands with arms folded and a knowing look. How grateful I am that my dad read me Thurber, otherwise I'd know nothing of these fables and have no suitable way to bide my time until our current nightmares tumble from a careless window." —Elvis Costello

"Every sport has its Ultimate, its Greatest of All Time: Babe Ruth, Ali, Nicklaus, Pelé, Federer, The Don. The sport of creating laugh-out-loud cartoons, fables, and funny essays has Thurber. He is, and probably always will be, The One." —Stephen Fry

"Thurber celebrates the losers, the awkward, the unpopular . . . and yet he's never a smug observer." —Tracey Ullman

"James Thurber taught me how to read. His pictures were so weirdly intriguing that I had to know more, so into the words I went, and things just got funnier. It's one of the longest and most important relationships in my reading life." —Michael McKean

"Thurber's genius was to make of our despair a humorous fable." —John Updike, 1956

"It was Whitman who wanted to turn and live with the animals; it is Thurber who has succeeded in the only possible terms, by enlisting them in the endless battle for human sanity."   —*Manchester Guardian* (London), 1957

"Take Aesop, or La Fontaine, add a dash of lunacy, garnish with the drawing of a man whose perfect vision is undistracted by good sight and you still won't have a Thurber fable . . . You won't have it because a Thurber fable is unique in the most unicorn sense of the word. A Thurber fable shares that special world of humor that we identify as Thurbeia, a wispy, wacky realm somewhere between heaven and mirth, inhabited by fierce, long-haired women, by apprehensive men whom life has passed by (and in the wrong direction at that), and by the hound dog of Idealism staring confounded at the bug of Reality."
                              —*Evening Citizen*, Ottawa, Canada, 1953

"These fables deliciously revise some of the well-known classic fables. They are illustrated by Mr. Thurber's incomparable—and I mean incomparable—drawings. For no one fills a few crude looking lines with more laughing gas than he does."   —*Chicago Tribune*, 1940

"These tiny stories, in which a wide variety of animals show us how human we really are, are completely uproarious."
                              —*Saturday Review of Literature*, 1940

"But Thurber, the fabulist, easily engages the invaluable services of Thurber, the scratch-pad artist. These ectoplasmic figures, seemingly executed in a telephone booth between wrong numbers, enhance his Fables more dynamically than the work of any other artist could, had he had a selection from Cimabue to Margaret Bourke-White. The little figures of animals and people depict every human mood save nobility and serenity. This is no lack, since there doesn't happen to be any serenity or nobility in the Fables."

—*Saturday Review*, 1956

"Thurber is an original. Critics who call him merely the Swift of our time underrate him, because he is something special, something all himself, as important a phenomenon of our time as the World's Fair or the World War. I wouldn't miss one of his books for anything. But I'm warning you, the laughs in this one are mostly desperate."

—*Memphis Tennessee Appeal*, 1940

"In Germany this Aesop in reverse would be burned at the stake as subversive, mad, immoral, decadent, and defeatist. He is also delightful."　　　　　—*The Nation*, 1940

"[Thurber] writes so simply and so pointedly that readers find it hard to believe that there isn't some esoteric meaning hidden under every word, and that his own illustrations—simple, often only one line drawings—are just what they look like and not a kind of ink curtain hiding all sorts of subtleties. You may not like him (though his devotees can't understand your having such a blind spot) but anyone who says he can't understand him is in a fog of his own making."

—*Chicago Sunday Tribune*, 1956

"[Thurber's fables] are spare, luminous, concentrated, they are Thurber's late quartets. His conflict has moved to a higher plane, it's no longer only man versus gadgets, or man versus woman. It's satire versus humanism; Thurber doesn't hate the human race, like Swift; he cares for it, and hopes, he has had a vision of paradise . . . But finally this is the distilled wisdom of the blind prophet."

—*Observer*, London, 1957

"So long as Mr. Thurber continues to people our darkness with these little doodles of his, we Americans are not much in danger of losing the uses of laughter."

—Buffalo, *NY News*, 1956

"Here Thurber energetically continues his huge self-assigned task of trying to kid mankind into taking itself seriously. And if he fails, it is only because mankind isn't listening."

—*Texas News*, Lufkin, 1957

"I always read my Thurber—to laugh and learn."

—Jon Scieszka

"I was introduced to Thurber in high school, and that's when I became a writer." —Roy Blount, Jr.

Collected Fables

BOOKS BY JAMES THURBER

A Mile and a Half of Lines:
The Art of James Thurber

The Thurber Letters

The Dog Department: James Thurber on Hounds,
Scotties, and Talking Poodles

People Have More Fun Than Anybody:
A Centennial Celebration of Drawings
and Writings by James Thurber

Collecting Himself:
James Thurber on Writing and
Writers, Humor and Himself

Selected Letters of James Thurber

Thurber & Company

A Thurber Carnival (a musical revue)

Credos and Curios

Lanterns and Lances

The Years with Ross

Alarms and Diversions

The Wonderful O

Further Fables for Our Time

Thurber's Dogs

Thurber Country

The Thurber Album: A Collection of Pieces About People

The 13 Clocks

The Beast in Me and Other Animals

Collected Fables

James Thurber

EDITED BY Michael J. Rosen
FOREWORD BY Keith Olbermann

HARPER**PERENNIAL** MODERN**CLASSICS**

NEW YORK • LONDON • TORONTO • SYDNEY • NEW DELHI • AUCKLAND

HARPER**PERENNIAL** ● MODERN**CLASSICS**

HarperCollins books may be purchased for educational, business, or sales promotional use. For information, please email the Special Markets Department at SPsales@harpercollins.com.

FIRST EDITION

Designed by Jen Overstreet

All Illustrations by James Thurber, except as noted:

"The Flaw in the Plan," (217) © 2019 Laurie Rosenwald
"A Farewell to Mandibles," (221) © 2019 Seymour Chwast
"Many Pigeons," (225) © 2019 Victoria Chess
"The Ordeal of No. 137,968," (227) and "The Pigeon Who Wouldn't Go Home,"
(235) © 2019 Victoria Roberts
"The Possum Who Wasn't Playing Dead," (239) © 2019 Mark Ulriksen
"The Starling and the Crow," (242) © 2019 Eric Hanson
"The Generalissimo of All the Field Mice in the World," (245) © 2019 Edel Rodriguez
"The Bright Emperor," (248) © 2019 R.O. Blechman
"The Princess and the Tin Box," (253) © 2019 Blair Thornley
"The Last Clock," (259) © 2019 Calef Brown

Library of Congress Cataloging-in-Publication Data has been applied for.

ISBN 978-0-06-290917-6

HB 09.07.2023

Contents

Foreword

Keith Olbermann

It doesn't come up in conversation much, but I have a tattoo on my right arm of a moth flying toward a star.

Obviously, James Thurber did not draw this on my arm and he certainly did not tattoo it there either, but nevertheless the Moth and the Star are his, in the same way that the Peacelike Mongoose is his and the Bear Who Let It Alone is his and the Unicorn in the Garden is his. They, and all his other animal stand-ins for the pageant of humans—brilliant and dim alike—are his, eternally, indelibly, and never to be duplicated. Of course, if you are really serious about Thurber's animals and the fables they populate, you can get tattoos. But as a first step I would recommend reading this first-ever, authoritative compilation of the fables. Tattoos can wait.*

But reading the fables can't. They remain startlingly appropriate to the human condition, and as someone who has read them for half a century and read them aloud for a decade, I can testify that they remain precisely relevant to the freshest political and cultural quicksand of each new year. We keep making the same mistakes, practically begging Thurber's Very Proper Gander and his Bat Who Got the Hell Out and his Chief of Police Dogs to keep rotating to the front of the stage to say, "We told you so."

I first tried to do verbal justice to Thurber's writing in 1979 as part of a public-speaking class in college. I had seen the great William Windom's one-man Thurber show on PBS, and in those pre-DVR (indeed, pre-VCR) days, I managed to record most of it on audiocassette. After I did a bad impression of Windom's spectacular interpretation, a classmate told me I should abandon my intended career in sports and newscasting and instead make my living by reading Thurber aloud. I said I'd be happy to but, all things considered, I was likelier to be asked to pay for the privilege than be paid for it.

I was finally proved wrong by the very person who had

---

*   Did I mention that my moth and star are part of a matching set? And that I've got an ex-girlfriend who has the moral from the same fable, "The Moth and the Star," tattooed onto her back? You think explaining a moth every once in a while is a task, try justifying *this* written on your skin—in italics, no less: *Moral: Who flies afar from the sphere of our sorrow is here today and here tomorrow.*

introduced me to Thurber: my father. During his last illness, I read to him every night in the hospital for seven months, and one night after I had read about twenty Thurber fables to him, he asked me to read "The Peacelike Mongoose" for a second time. He then told me to stop for a moment, and after long thought he said, "You should do that in your newscast." I said that didn't seem to make sense and besides, there were copyrights and such to worry about. That's when my dad said, "How many times have I ever suggested anything to you about your shows?" I couldn't recall him ever having done so. "Try it," he said. "What's the worst that can happen?" He slipped into a coma not long after, and in his honor I went on television and read "The Peacelike Mongoose."

His conviction that reading the story would appeal to my audience was correct. The ratings went up, and soon the Thurber segments became the most-watched quarter-hour on MSNBC every Friday. But my conviction that reading the story would precipitate a proprietary response from Thurber's literary estate was also right.

The email arrived within days of my reading "The Peacelike Mongoose"—but it bore no resemblance to my fears. Instead it contained a story from two of my regular viewers about how they had been wrestling with an impossible dilemma over that very fable. They had been approached by a publisher who wanted to include "The Peacelike Mongoose" in a textbook—but only if they agreed to remove one word. The two viewers? James Thurber's daughter, Rosemary, and his granddaughter, Sara Thurber Sauers. And the worrisome word? One entirely and deliciously of Thurber's creation: *mongoosexual*.

Nothing Thurber ever wrote was a throwaway or designed to be edited a half century later. Rosemary Thurber would testify to her father's daylong agonies over whether the comma should go after the fourth word of the thirty-third sentence or after the fifth. He wrote—or as his vision vanished, he dictated—each word and punctuation mark to be published as planned. In "The Peacelike Mongoose" he wrote *mongoosexual* and he meant *mongoosexual*.

Thurber's immediate fame continued after his death in 1961, extended into the seventies and eighties by those who had grown up with him, and then into the nineties, as scholars began to analyze his work and chronicle his life in biographies. But by 2010, when I first read Thurber on my show, his work had fallen into an inevitable dormancy, and the time was ripe for rediscovery. Should Rosemary Thurber really keep her father out of a textbook and out of the minds of a generation of potential new addicts just because of one word?

And then I said that word on national television, and Sara phoned her mother and said, "I think you have your answer," and sure enough, they told the publishers to print the story intact or not at all—and they printed it intact!

And there began my formal association with Thurber and the weekly readings on television and online, and as a consequence, the Thurber renaissance transpired a little earlier than expected, and his collections and fables began appearing on Amazon's "Movers & Shakers" list, and then two reprints of the Library of America edition of *Thurber*, and then an audiobook they let me perform, and then theatrical advice from William Windom. And ultimately, that tattoo.

The late Mr. Windom agreed that Thurber's unique status as the Babe Ruth of twentieth-century humor is probably best expressed in the fables. Remarkably, there is almost no "bad" Thurber, though the short stories often ask a lot from a reader, and the drawings are often simultaneously perfect and yet leave one hungering for the backstory. The fables, on the other hand, combine the best of Thurber the writer and Thurber the artist. The moral that concludes each one underscores Thurber's intent, and the consistent Aesop-like length permits the reader to anticipate exactly when the payoff of insight and humor or outrage will hit.

They are also delights to read aloud. I firmly recommend that you try this, even if you're alone. Thurber did not write to be performed, but there is no mistaking the instincts of the old college thespian and the later Broadway playwright— they resonate in every line.

If you are in a buoyant mood, you can hear in every anthropomorphic character or see in every Thurber illustration the joy of a life well laughed. If you are less sanguine, you can sense the existential threat of "the claw of the sea-puss"* that gets us all in the end. But either way, you can feel what he felt in his heart—good, bad, but never indifferent. It mattered to him, it moved him, it maddened him, it made him laugh, and he was able to refine it and convey it and leave it for us in a manner no one else has ever done.

---

*   Ed. Note: The ring of that phrase is so "deliciously" Thurberesque, as Mr. Olbermann undoubtedly relishes . . . even as Thurber did. Thurber's preface to *My Life and Hard Times* ends, "It is unfortunate, however, that even a well-ordered life cannot lead anybody safely around the inevitable doom that waits in the skies. As F. Hopkinson Smith long ago pointed out, the claw of the sea-puss gets us all in the end." (The phrase is a chapter title from Smith's romance, *The Tides of Barnegat*, published when Thurber was twelve, in 1906. As for "sea-puss"? Derived from the native Algonquian languages, it refers to a strong undertow or riptide rushing seaward.)

Finally, there is the matter of new Thurber material: a preface and ten fables that never appeared in his books, along with lovingly created new illustrations by other artists that add to the sheer joy of Thurber's original work, like a lemon twist or just the right nightcap.

On the subject of newness, I am delighted to admit that when asked to perform the fable "The Flaw in the Plan" at an event in New York, I knowingly and accommodatingly nodded, and then as soon as I was by myself, I said aloud, "The Flaw in the Plan"? What the hell is "The Flaw in the Plan"? I never read anything by Thurber called "The Flaw in the Plan"! The manuscript of this book quickly arrived and I was overwhelmed to learn that there was yet another Thurber fable to enjoy, as topical as if it had been written yesterday. There are fables here that you have never read before! Thus, if you are encountering some, many, or all of these fables for the first time, I envy you. Please relish your rapture and remember that this way lies tattoos.

A Fabulist for *Our* Time

From his early stories and cartoons in that nascent magazine, *The New Yorker*, to the last works dictated before his death in late 1961, James Thurber negotiated a terrain that was as confounding as it was recognizably our own—most often, in the role of fabulist.

Thurber's works were and are the product of a mind bent over backward to make sense—or even nonsense—of a chaotic world. Their range is especially broad, from stories such as the renowned "The Secret Life of Walter Mitty," to his suite of boyhood memories *My Life and Hard Times* (a book Russell Baker said was "possibly the shortest and most elegant autobiography ever written"[*]); from his broadly appealing books for

---

[*]   Baker, Russell. From the afterword of *My Life and Hard Times* by James Thurber. New York Times Co., 1989. Reprinted by Harper Perennial Classics, 1999.

younger readers, to his reminiscences of the familiar figures of his youth (*The Thurber Album*) or his colleagues at *The New Yorker* (*The Years with Ross*). And to this we must add his voluminous work as a cartoonist and illustrator.

"If you're like me, and I know I am . . ." was Thurber's quintessential perspective. He was an acutely, if not painfully, perceptive man, and he counted that on some deep level, the irritation he perceived wasn't merely a personal pettiness but was, in fact, something rampant in the general population. The blasts of bafflement that chilled Thurber to the bone often became more than cocktail banter: more like battle cries in a common outrage. Thurber used humor to dance through life, offering himself up quite seriously as laughing matter as he shimmied under the lower and lower pole of the ideal.

Humor is the midpoint between boorishly whining and feverishly declaiming, between "woe is me" and "listen to me!" It's an attempt at equilibrium and homeostasis—that survival strategy that requires the least expenditure of energy for the maximum necessary comfort. Throughout much of his prose, Thurber shrewdly focused on being a human *animal*, an adaptable being among other beasts. (Indeed, he once considered "The Bestiary in Me" as title for one of his collections.) As the *Manchester Guardian* wrote of his fables: "It was Whitman who wanted to turn and live with the animals; it is Thurber who has succeeded in the only possible terms, by enlisting them in the endless battle for human sanity."

And so we find Thurber's humor often constructed at the intersection of *really?* and reality. Bridging such discrepancy, his dreamed-up outcomes lean on the signpost alongside present dramas. *That way*, one is moving toward the choreography of an imagined future. *This way*, one sees the muddy footprints of foreclosed facts. Thurber's pages braid sobering facts and drunken hopes into a thread, a tightrope that spanned the abyss—this abysmal span of his then-current events.

The fables are thus quintessential Thurber, a distillation, a coup de grâce that share his best cartoons' puissance: not just "ha ha," but "aha."

Despite the decades that have passed since their composition, the eighty-five fables collected here possess a renewed relevance in this "Life and Hard Times" of ours. Partly, it's the timeless nature of fables themselves. They're pastoral windows that exist both within and beyond a particular time. Most of Thurber's preoccupations, the subjects that pricked and prodded him throughout his various books, are reprised and distilled in these short works with wizened authority: the untidy course of love; the bitterness of lost hope; false speech and the loosening grip on language; mistrust and suspiciousness; the mongering of hate and the fragility of peace. All these topics are at the core of these miniature narratives.

A fable may be spare in its form, but not in its complexity of ideas, personalities, politics, and applicability. Only a writer of formidable talent can concoct an utterly modest realm, populate it with simple characters (animals, principally), juxtapose their primal motives and conflicts, and craft a work that, much the way a prism separates light into its elemental parts, clarifies a spectrum of our truest natures from the blurriness of daily life.

Between the writing of *Fables for Our Time and Famous Poems Illustrated* (1940) and *Further Fables for Our Time* (1956), two factors altered the character of Thurber's work. His vision failed. The sight in his right eye that had been progressively diminishing since the bow-and-arrow incident took his left eye in his childhood finally prevented Thurber from seeing at all. Prior to the 1940s, he was able to create the cartoons, illustrations, advertising campaigns, and children's books with pen and ink. But after a series of difficult and not entirely successful eye operations in 1941, the remaining vision in his right eye clouded and rendered him blind.

Various biographers and critics have suggested that his partial sight invited more fantasy into his perceived reality—mistaken perceptions whose creative potential Thurber often exploited.

Likewise, the auditory nature of his work—particularly the fables—increased considerably as Thurber wrote and rewrote the latter fables in his head, polishing passages until each became a cabochon of grammatical finesse, coruscating wordplay, and aural antics. The renowned critic Malcolm Cowley's review of *Further Fables for Our Time* suggested that Thurber created "a completely verbalized universe." Critic David McCord called this "American original" "a wild tyrannothesaurus type when on the hunt for words."[*]

The other significant change simply coincided with America's postwar climate: the "dark national weather" as Thurber called it, of the Great War, postwar years, and the McCarthy era of distrust, suspicion, and conformity.

Gerald Weales, in a lengthy review in *Commonweal*, notes that Thurber's "fifteen-year journey from *Fables for Our Time* (1940) to *Further Fables for Our Time*" reflects "a kind of escape

---

[*]   McCord, David. *Twentieth Century Children's Writers*, 4th ed., edited by Laura Standley Berger. Farmingham, Mich.: St. James Press, 1995.

from a world that was becoming increasingly difficult to face."* And he cites Thurber's biographical recollections—*The Thurber Album* and *The Years with Ross*—and his children's books—*Many Moons*, *The Great Quillow*, *The White Deer*, and *The 13 Clocks*—as the more comfortable detours he published in this period.

In an interview just before his fifty-fifth birthday, Thurber described another of the many projects in the switching yard of his bustling mind. He was hard upon a more extended fable such as "The Last Clock," featured in this book: "The Spoodle," a parable of confusion running some twelve thousand words.

"The story is placed in a country called Confusia. In it, everybody is suspected of the wrong thing. One person has seen the spoodle, another has heard it, and a third has even tasted it. The prosecutor is sure that the spoodle is un-Confusian and has to find it. If he can't find one, the prosecutor says, he will have to build one. It's a satire on the Un-American Committee's worst confusions."†

It's the return to the fables that provided Thurber a plainspoken, accessible, and satiric way to "protest against the American assault on its own culture."‡ And it's our return to them—collected here with several that have never seen the printed page—that proves his fables as cogent and necessary today as they were in his era of uneasiness and uncertainty. These fables are, indeed, for *our* time.

---

*   Weales, Gerald. *Commonweal*, January 18, 1957.

†   Breit, Harvey. "Mr. Thurber observes a serene birthday." *New York Times Magazine*, Dec. 4, 1949.

‡   Letter to William Faulkner, October 2, 1956, from *The Thurber Letters*, edited by Harrison Kinney with Rosemary A. Thurber (New York: Simon & Schuster, 2002), 663.

A Note About the Contents

All the fables in *Fables for Our Time*, along with Thurber's accompanying drawings, first appeared in *The New Yorker* during 1939 and 1940. The collection, published as a single volume by Harper & Brothers in 1940, included some alternate versions of drawings, as well as Thurber's "Famous Poems Illustrated," a suite of nine treasured poems of the era.

Of the forty-seven fables in *Further Fables for Our Time*, ten did not appear in *The New Yorker* prior to book publication by Harper & Brothers in 1956: "The Sea and the Shore," "The Lion and the Foxes," "The Hen Party," "The Bears and the Monkeys," "The Chipmunk and His Mate," "The Trial of the Old Watchdog," "The Godfather and His Godchild," "Tea for One," "The Lady of the Legs," and "The Shore and the Sea."

The line drawings for Thurber's second fable collection were all adapted from miscellaneous illustrations Thurber had completed before blindness overtook both eyes. The majority of his pen-and-ink work ceased by 1940; until 1950 or so, he occasionally tried a broader pencil or chalk on poster-size sheets of paper . . . and even used white chalk on black paper that the printer would reverse before printing. Most of the *Further Fables* images were selected from larger drawings, shrunk, enlarged, or otherwise manipulated, and assigned to one or another fable. It is not known what role Thurber, his wife Helen, or the publisher's editor or designer had in selecting and presenting the drawings.

The continued archiving and cataloging of Thurber's art by both the Thurber Estate and The Ohio State University Rare Books and Manuscripts Library provided renewed options for illustrating *Further Fables for Our Time* that better maintain the integrity of Thurber's line quality and more aptly match the fables' subject matter.

Of the fables that were never collected in a book prior to *Collected Fables*, three were published in *The New Yorker*. "The Bright Emperor" (August 20, 1932); "The Princess and the Tin Box" (September 29, 1945, subsequently included in Thurber's collection *The Beast in Me and Other Animals*, 1948); and the late, lengthy tale, "The Last Clock" (February 21, 1959, and included in *Lanterns and Lances*, a collection published months before his death in November 1961).

Among the folders of Thurber's manuscripts is a collection of fables in various states of composition. Some exist in multiple drafts such as "The Hepcat and the Barkeep (A Fable in Animal Slang)," an aural feat that I sense would fall on mostly deaf ears in this era (i.e., "If you can't outfox that mouse, you're a pussycat. Give her a cock-and-bull story. Tell her you were skylarking and fell among wolves. Don't sing your swan song like a lame duck, and stop drinking like a fish.").

Some of the folder's pages are little more than notes: a title such as "The Cardinal and the Turtle," followed by a working paragraph or two. (This one happens to contain this zinger: "'You look like an accident coming back from where it happened,' said the cardinal. 'I get along,' said the turtle.") A few sheets have titles and morals waiting for a story such as, "This we all should learn and teach, loose talk is not free speech."

It's worth pointing out that for the last two decades of his life, Thurber composed in one of two ways: by scrawling increasingly large and fewer words on stacks of typing paper that his wife or secretary would transcribe, or by dictating from memory. He could write and revise upwards of three thousand words in his head and then recite them to be typed. Even so, Thurber still had little means of revisiting and reviewing all that he continued to create unless he specifically recalled it and had it read back to him.

It's the ongoing consideration of Thurber's canon over the last thirty-five years—a partnership I've had the honor to undertake with James's daughter, Rosemary Thurber, his granddaughter, Sara Thurber Sauers, and the Estate's literary agent, Barbara Hogenson—that has prompted the inclusion of the following seven fables: "The Flaw in the Plan," "The Starling and the Crow," "The Possum Who Wasn't Playing Dead," "A Farewell to Mandibles," an incomplete draft of "The Generalissimo of All the Field Mice in the World," and three versions of another fable: "Many Pigeons," "The Ordeal of No. 137,968," and "The Pigeon Who Wouldn't Go Home."

The year 2019 is the 125th anniversary of James Thurber's birth. As such, his hometown of Columbus, Ohio, has designated it as "The Year of Thurber"—an occasion to acquaint or reacquaint readers with Thurber's canon. One major event will be an exhibition of his artwork at The Columbus Museum of Art (August 2019 until March 2020). It's to be accompanied by a monograph, *A Mile and a Half of Lines: The Art of James Thurber*, that will feature some 250 drawings, a third of which have never been published.

This volume of fables, likewise, offers a chance to show Thurber's continuing influence on contemporary artists: *New Yorker* cartoonists and beyond. It's key to pause here, and remember that it was Thurber who instrumentally shifted the cartoon's nature from being an artfully drawn depiction of a humorous situation or observation with some commentary or badinage, into an article of humor itself: the lines themselves, both drawn and written, were the humor. It was Thurber who invited spontaneity, unpremeditated compositions, and a style of drawing that had little to do with accuracy, preliminary sketches, or training. As veteran *New Yorker* cartoonist Michael Maslin has written, "Thurber's drawings dropped into the pages of *The New Yorker* like graphic boulders in a placid pond."

The ten contemporary artists and cartoonists invited to illustrate Thurber's works here all credit Thurber as an inspiration or influence. Their works are a championing chorus that proves the endurance of Thurber's line—both the physical line on the page as well as the lineage of his genius that continues to liberate and excite new creators in the graphic arts.

—MICHAEL J. ROSEN

Collected Fables

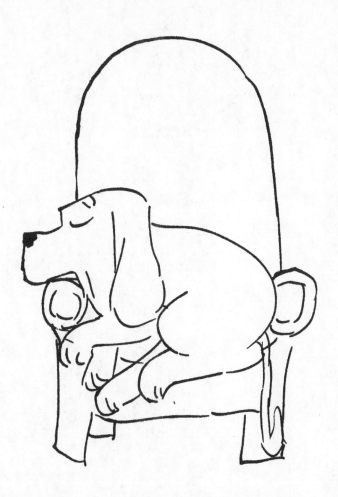

Preface

The human family, of which I am a sometimes reluctant, but often proud, member, has always invited a story, resented a lecture, and yawned at a sermon—as La Fontaine put it—while needing all three, and so the literature of our surprisingly extant species is a history of the fine art of making the three voices speak with one tongue. This synchronizing can be traced, if you have an idle year on your hands, all the way from the pre-Christian fables that warned men of the traps and pitfalls of their follies and passions, up to today's singing commercials, which tell people how happiness can be brought to the home through the use of mild detergents, or by the smoking of cigarettes. The ancient apologues, to use a neatly alliterative academic

---

Ed. Note: Thurber wrote this preface for *Further Fables for Our Time*, but it was not originally published with the collection.

synonym I kept stumbling over while browsing in the ver-
biage of literary historians, are not only wiser, but easier to
listen to than the other genre. I can follow pretty well most
of the simpler Latin fables, when they are read aloud, but it
took me three weeks to make out what it was the little girls
were saying in the Contadina Tomato Paste* commercial,
although the lyric seemed to be written in English.

Fable production, as marketing statisticians would call
it, by which I mean the turning out of new fables in told
traditional form, has fallen off in our time about as much
as the production of wood burning sets or surrey fringe.
Most literary formulas thrive best in the climate of their
particular periods, and this was true of the fables of Aesop, the early Romans, and the medieval French and Brah-
mins. You come out of the dusty alcoves of fables, coughing
from stuffiness, confusion, and the contrary speculations of
scholars, and the experience gives you a perverse desire to
throw around some conjectures and generalizations of your
own, or at least it gave me one. If you will kindly not scrape
your chairs, I shall get through with this prefatoration (my
own classical word) in nearly no time at all. Twenty-five
centuries ago, fables were made in order to shorten a journey, lighten a burden, amuse a monarch, instruct a class,
comfort or exhort a friend, mock a tyrant, or society itself,
in a kind of metaphorical cipher code, harangue, or, best of
all, please the narrator himself.

Fables, in their genuine state, were as popular with
ancient slaves and freedom, patricians and philosophers,

---

* "Who put eight great tomatoes in that little bitty can?" A series of
radio spots by Stan Freberg from 1956.

kings and commoners as bleated love songs, gooey with ungrammatical yearning, are popular today among teenagers and emotionally underprivileged adults. The mistaken idea that fables were originally for children has bored children for a good thousand years, and nowadays they shiver a bit in the austere presence of Aesop, however big the type or gaudy the colored illustrations, as they would shiver in the cold interior of a Gothic summer house. If Jean de La Fontaine, of Paris, Château-Thierry, and the seventeenth century, greatest of the translators and adaptors of fables, had not given them a new light touch, they might have died out of modern languages some two hundred and thirty years before the invention of the teddy bear.

Literature owes a great debt to La Fontaine, surely the most translated poet since Horace, for the liveliness he brought to a staid old pattern. He didn't take to fables, at first, like a duck to water, but more like a man to a dentist's chair, as far as I can make out, and if this old pious believer in precept and precedent had not found authority for liveliness of narration in Quintilian, he might not have done his famous tales. Old Quintilian, it seems, had once observed that liveliness is good for narratives. Now, millions of children and adults can recite La Fontaine's fables of the grasshopper and the ant, and the fox and the crow, and these and the others have been translated by everybody from God Knows Who to the Pulitzer Prize–winning poet Marianne Moore.

La Fontaine, who always had a child audience in mind (after all, fables have been used as textbooks for at least eighteen hundred years) takes a mild, but violent, liberty with the one about the fox and the grapes. He gives the frustrated fox a touch of philosophy, almost of benign resignation, making him out neither a complainer nor a whimperer. Fortunately, the power of old Aesop has outlived the Frenchman's tampering. The Fox is the sly rascal of Fable, and one of the great whiners in the history of words, and nobody can change him and nobody ought to try, for Reynard's place in Story is as firmly founded as Man's. Might as well try to make the kingly lion cowardly, like L. Frank Baum's in *The Wizard of Oz* or the ass a creature of discernment and wisdom.

If you really want to have a lot of turgid and exasperating fun, plunge into the cloistered comparative definitions of apologue, myth, allegory, folklore, parable, fairy tale, nursery rhyme, and proverb. You will come out of it babbling. The Britannica, for instance, opines that a proverb is a fossilized fable. Nonsense, gentlemen, the proverb is a distinct literary form, at its best and purest, as different from a fable as an arrow from an arquebus.* To be sure, you can take a proverb and write a fable around it, and many fabulists have, but such proverbs as "It's a long lane that has no turning," and "If wishes were horses beggars would ride," need a narrative context about as much as Dulles needs a kiddy car. Fossilized fables, if there are any, turn up in such play titles as "The Lion and the Mouse" and "The Cat and the Canary," and in detached Aesopian phrases like "the lion's share" and "sour grapes"—to get back to that fox. When the Colonel's lady and Judy say "sour grapes" they imply, properly, a feigned scorn for the unattainable, and flat contempt for those who

---

* The forerunner of the rifle; a muzzle-loaded firearm held against the shoulder.

can attain it. "The lion's share" is fossilized to the extent that it no longer means all of anything, but merely the larger part of it, when it is mentioned by the Colonel or by Judy's man. It may fall to dust before long, or gain a revived currency, depending on how Man comes out in the war against Himself. The dusty definitionizers, by the way, probably caused Horace's fable of the country mouse and the city mouse to fall into nursery tales, and out of fables except when only the scene in the house of the city mouse is used. Horace, who got it from a neighbor, who had heard it from an old woman, put it down in two scenes, beginning with the one in the house of the country mouse. To the academicians this violates a misguided feeling for the unities of time and space. The definition of fables should not be cramped. There is only one valid recipe and it is simple. Take a pointed and recognizable aspect of human behavior, stir it up with talking animals or trees or persons or piggy banks or anything else, and turn it out in a concentrated narrative. Cover with sauce a la maison, piquant or didactic, sardonic, saturnine, sarcastic, sanguine, or any other kind except pedantic and pontifical. Serve sparingly. Fables should be consumed a few at a time, like oysters, or perhaps even chocolate nut sundaes. Add, of course, a twist of moral, which can come anywhere, or, for that matter, nowhere: as topic sentence, final rhyme, stuck in the middle, or merely implied.

Americans, and Englishmen, too, have rarely been very good at the conventional fable formula that scholars love so well, although the English have always had a great skill in legend, folklore, nursery rhyme, and the Goldilocks kind of animal story, and the American air and printed page are filled with informal types of fables: Brer Rabbit, the tall tale, the animated apologues starring Donald Duck and his circle, the recent natural history of animals by Disney and others, such truly authentic fables, rhymed and set to music, as "Rudolf the Red-Nosed Reindeer" and "Barney the Bashful Bullfrog," and sharpest and closest of all, the shaggy dog stories.

The original shaggy dog story—where it actually started I don't know—is familiar to young and old. It could be adorned offhand with half a dozen morals by any fabulist of the great tradition. The version I know goes like this. A Londoner advertises in the newspapers for his lost dog, describing its looks, and emphasizing its shagginess. An American in New York—or Nashville or San Diego—reads the ad in a paper he picks up in a bar, and shortly afterward encounters a remarkably shaggy dog in his neighborhood, which seems to fit perfectly the description of the lost canine, so the finder boards a ship, taking the dog with him, and knocks at last upon the door of the house in London. It is opened by the bereft advertiser who glances at the dog the American has brought him, and says, "Oh, but it wasn't that shaggy."

The best American narrator of fables in the historic manner of old Aesop himself, was, in my unhumble opinion, the late Bob Burns of Radio's old Kraft Music Hall. His finest fable, and if you ever heard it you will never forget it, dealt with a little boy and his father and a turtle. The little boy finds his pet motionless and apparently dead in its pan of water and is inconsolable. Neither his mother nor a child psychiatrist who is called in can comfort him, and they finally send for his father (the father was Bing Crosby and the little boy his son Lindsay in the Burns tale, because Crosby was also a Kraft entertainer at the time). The father tells his son that he will place the small turtle in a silver cigarette case, and bury it in a special private grave, complete with tiny head-stone, just under the boy's bedroom window, and arrange to have it light up when the child flicks a switch beside his bed at night. And so the father and his son went out into the kitchen to get the turtle, but they found it swimming about in its pan, not dead at all, but healthy as life itself. And the little boy looked up at his father and said, "Let's kill him."

America's one immortal written fable, I think, is Mark Twain's episode of the two boys and the fence that has to be whitewashed. This situation pops up here and there in the literature of ye olde apologues, but Samuel Clemens did it better than any of the old professional fable writer. There have been other American fabulists, of course, and everybody of my advance years knows about George Ade's experiments in putting fables into slang. The best of recent native fabu-lists was the late, neglected William March, mainly known for his novel *Company K* and the more recent *The Bad Seed*, on which the Broadway play of the same name is based. A dozen of his sharply sardonic fables are included in a volume called *A William March Omnibus*, but he must have written at least thirty others. They appeared in the *New York Post*, where they were almost as invisible as top secret documents in Washington.

Nothing called a fable was ever less like a fable than Wil-liam Faulkner's *A Fable*. Hemingway's *The Old Man and the Sea*, on the other hand, is a fable in everything except length. The definition of a fable shouldn't be cramped. It can em-brace any pointed and recognizable aspect of human behavior, turned out in a concentrated narrative, with birds and beasts, or people or chimney posts, or anything else, including parts of the human body, talking away at a great rate. Old Horace wrote a deathless fable, the one about the country mouse and the city mouse, but you usually find it only in nursery tales in its original form.

(Incidentally, I wrote a series of unfabulous pieces for the *Post* about 1927, warning that the city's water supply would be in a critical state in 1952 or thereabouts, and I darn near hit it on the head. These pieces didn't help any, however, because they are probably the least known of any series of articles in the history of the journalistic world.)

I am happy to have got through this without a single footnote, or the use of such formidable quotations, however apropos as *arbores loquuntur, non tantum ferae.*[*]

This brings us to a few little old new fables of my own. I'm not sure whether they are oysters, or chocolate nut sundaes, or what. That is up to the definitionizers, or such of them as may still be alive and interested.

—JAMES THURBER
MARCH 30, 1956

---

[*] The Latin translates as "talking trees, not only in the wild." Thurber is citing Phaedrus's *Prologue* to his fables. Or perhaps Dr. Johnson's use of it in his *Life of Gay*, in which he posits: "A fable or apologue seems to be, in its genuine state, a narrative in which beings irrational, and sometimes inanimate (*arbores loquuntur, non tantum ferae*) are, for the purposes of moral instruction, feigned to act and speak with human interest and passions."

This book's original dedication read, "For Herman and Dorothy."

The Mouse Who Went
to the Country

ONCE UPON A SUNDAY there was a city mouse who went to visit a country mouse. He hid away on a train the country mouse had told him to take, only to find that on Sundays it did not stop at Beddington. Hence the city mouse could not get off at Beddington and catch a bus for Sibert's Junction, where he was to be met by the country mouse. The city mouse, in fact, was carried on to Middleburg, where he waited three hours for a train to take him back. When he got back to Beddington he found that the last bus for Sibert's Junction had just left, so he ran and he ran and he ran and he finally caught the bus and crept aboard, only to find that it was not the bus for Sibert's Junction at all, but was going in the opposite direction through Pell's Hollow and Grumm to a place called Wimberby. When the bus finally stopped, the city mouse got out into a heavy rain and found that there were no more buses that night going anywhere. "To the hell with it," said the city mouse, and he walked back to the city.

MORAL: *Stay where you are, you're sitting pretty.*

The Little Girl
and the Wolf

O NE AFTERNOON a big wolf waited in a dark forest for a little girl to come along carrying a basket of food to her grandmother. Finally a little girl did come along and she was carrying a basket of food. "Are you carrying that basket to your grandmother?" asked the wolf. The little girl said yes, she was. So the wolf asked her where her grandmother lived and the little girl told him and he disappeared into the wood.

When the little girl opened the door of her grandmother's house she saw that there was somebody in bed with a nightcap and nightgown on. She had approached no nearer than twenty-five feet from the bed when she saw that it was not her grandmother but the wolf, for even in a nightcap a wolf does not look any more like your grandmother than the Metro-Goldwyn lion looks like Calvin Coolidge. So the little girl took an automatic out of her basket and shot the wolf dead.

MORAL: *It is not so easy to fool little girls nowadays as it used to be.*

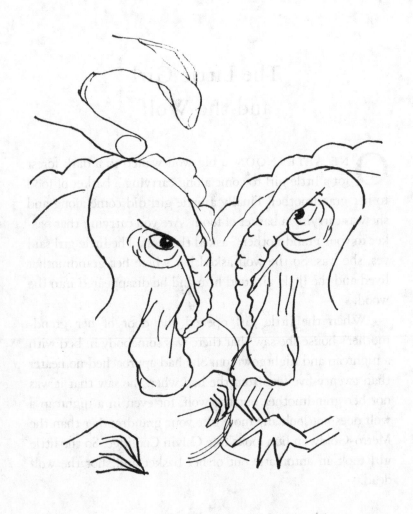

The Two Turkeys

ONCE UPON A TIME there were two turkeys, an old turkey and a young turkey. The old turkey had been cock of the walk for many years and the young turkey wanted to take his place. "I'll knock that old buzzard cold one of these days," the young turkey told his friends. "Sure you will, Joe, sure you will," his friends said, for Joe was treating them to some corn he had found. Then the friends went and told the old turkey what the young turkey had said. "Why, I'll have his gizzard!" said the old turkey, setting out some corn for his visitors. "Sure you will, Doc, sure you will," said the visitors.

One day the young turkey walked over to where the old turkey was telling tales of his prowess in battle. "I'll bat your teeth into your crop," said the young turkey. "You and who else?" said the old turkey. So they began to circle around each other, sparring for an opening. Just then the farmer who owned the turkeys swept up the young one and carried him off and wrung his neck.

MORAL: *Youth will be served, frequently stuffed with chestnuts.*

The Tiger Who
Understood People

O NCE UPON A TIME there was a tiger who escaped from a zoo in the United States and made
his way back to the jungle. During his captivity the tiger
had learned a great deal about how men do things and he
thought he would apply their methods to life in the jungle.
The first day he was home he met a leopard and he said,
"There's no use in you and me hunting for food; we'll make
the other animals bring it to us." "How will we do that?"
asked the leopard. "Easy," said the tiger, "you and I will tell
everybody that we are going to put on a fight and that every
animal will have to bring a freshly killed boar in order to
get in and see the fight. Then we will just spar around and
not hurt each other. Later you can say you broke a bone in
your paw during the second round and I will say I broke
a bone in my paw during the first round. Then we will
announce a return engagement and they'll have to bring
us more wild boars." "I don't think this will work," said
the leopard. "Oh, yes it will," said the tiger. "You just go
around saying that you can't help winning because I am a
big palooka and I will go around saying I can't lose because

you are a big palooka, and everybody will want to come and see the fight."

So the leopard went around telling everybody that he couldn't help winning because the tiger was a big palooka and the tiger went around telling everybody he couldn't lose because the leopard was a big palooka. The night of the fight came and the tiger and the leopard were very hungry because they hadn't gone out and done any hunting at all; they wanted to get the fight over as soon as possible and eat some of the freshly killed wild boars which all the animals would bring to the fight. But when the hour of the combat came none of the animals at all showed up. "The way I look at it," a fox had told them, "is this: if the leopard can't help winning and the tiger can't lose, it will be a draw and a draw is a very dull thing to watch, particularly when fought by fighters who are both big palookas." The animals all saw the logic of this and stayed away from the arena. When it got to be midnight and it was obvious that none of the animals would appear and that there wouldn't be any wild-boar meat to devour, the tiger and the leopard fell upon each other in a rage. They were both injured so badly and they were both so worn out by hunger that a couple of wild boars who came wandering along attacked them and killed them easily.

MORAL: *If you live as humans do, it will be the end of you.*

The Fairly
Intelligent
Fly

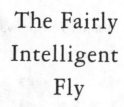

A LARGE SPIDER
in an old house
built a beautiful web
in which to catch
flies. Every time a fly
landed on the web and
was entangled in it the
spider devoured him, so
that when another fly came
along he would think the
web was a safe and quiet place
in which to rest. One day a fairly
intelligent fly buzzed around above the
web so long without lighting that the spider appeared and
said, "Come on down." But the fly was too clever for him
and said, "I never light where I don't see other flies and I
don't see any other flies in your house." So he flew away until he came to a place where there were a great many other

19

flies. He was about to settle down among them when a bee
buzzed up and said, "Hold it, stupid, that's flypaper. All those
flies are trapped." "Don't be silly," said the fly, "they're dancing." So he settled down and became stuck to the flypaper
with all the other flies.

MORAL: *There is no safety in numbers, or in anything else.*

The Lion Who Wanted to Zoom

THERE WAS ONCE a lion who coveted an eagle's wings. So he sent a message to the eagle asking him to call, and when the eagle came to the lion's den the lion said, "I will trade you my mane for your wings." "Keep talking, brother," said the

21

eagle. "Without my wings I could no longer fly." "So what?" said the lion. "I can't fly now, but that doesn't keep me from being king of beasts. I became king of beasts on account of my magnificent mane." "All right," said the eagle, "but give me your mane first." "Just approach a little nearer," said the lion, "so that I can hand it to you." The eagle came closer and the lion clapped a huge paw on him, pinning him to the ground. "Come across with those wings!" he snarled.

So the lion took the eagle's wings but kept his own mane. The eagle was very despondent for a while and then he had an idea. "I bet you can't fly off the top of that great rock yonder," said the eagle. "Who, me?" said the lion, and he walked to the top of the rock and took off. His weight was too great for the eagle's wings to support, and besides he did not know how to fly, never having tried it before. So he crashed at the foot of the rock and burst into flames. The eagle hastily climbed down to him and regained his wings and took off the lion's mane, which he put about his own neck and shoulders. Flying back to the rocky nest where he lived with his mate, he decided to have some fun with her. So, covered with the lion's mane, he poked his head into the nest and in a deep, awful voice said, "Harrrooo!" His mate, who was very nervous anyway, grabbed a pistol from a bureau drawer and shot him dead, thinking he was a lion.

MORAL: *Never allow a nervous female to have access to a pistol, no matter what you're wearing.*

The Very Proper Gander

NOT SO VERY long ago there was a very fine gander. He was strong and smooth and beautiful and he spent most of his time singing to his wife and children. One day somebody who saw him strutting up and down in his yard and singing remarked, "There is a very proper gander." An old hen overheard this and told her husband about it that night in the roost. "They said something about propaganda," she said. "I have always suspected that," said the rooster, and he went around the barnyard next day telling everybody that the very fine gander was a dangerous bird, more than likely a hawk in gander's clothing. A small brown hen remembered a time when at a great distance she had seen the gander talking with some hawks in the forest. "They were up to no good," she said. A duck remembered that the gander had once told him he did not believe in anything. "He said to hell with the flag, too," said the duck. A guinea hen recalled that she had once seen somebody who looked very much like the gander throw something that looked a great deal like a bomb. Finally everybody snatched up sticks and stones and descended on the gander's house. He was strutting in his front yard, singing to his children and his wife. "There he is!" everybody cried. "Hawk-lover! Unbeliever! Flag-hater! Bomb-thrower!" So they set upon him and drove him out of the country.

MORAL: *Anybody who you or your wife thinks is going to overthrow the government by violence must be driven out of the country.*

The Moth and the Star

A YOUNG AND IMPRESSIONABLE moth once set his
heart on a certain star. He told his mother about this
and she counselled him to set his heart on a bridge lamp instead. "Stars aren't the thing to hang around," she said; "lamps

are the thing to hang around." "You get somewhere that way," said the moth's father. "You don't get anywhere chasing stars." But the moth would not heed the words of either parent. Every evening at dusk when the star came out he would start flying toward it and every morning at dawn he would crawl back home worn out with his vain endeavor. One day his father said to him, "You haven't burned a wing in months, boy, and it looks to me as if you were never going to. All your brothers have been badly burned flying around street lamps and all your sisters have been terribly singed flying around house lamps. Come on, now, get out of here and get yourself scorched! A big strapping moth like you without a mark on him!"

The moth left his father's house, but he would not fly around street lamps and he would not fly around house lamps. He went right on trying to reach the star, which was four and one-third light years, or twenty-five trillion miles, away. The moth thought it was just caught in the top branches of an elm. He never did reach the star, but he went right on trying, night after night, and when he was a very, very old moth he began to think that he really had reached the star and he went around saying so. This gave him a deep and lasting pleasure, and he lived to a great old age. His parents and his brothers and his sisters had all been burned to death when they were quite young.

MORAL: *Who flies afar from the sphere of our sorrow is here today and here tomorrow.*

The Shrike
and the Chipmunks

ONCE UPON A TIME there were two chipmunks, a male and a female. The male chipmunk thought that arranging nuts in artistic patterns was more fun than just piling them up to see how many you could pile up. The female was all for piling up as many as you could. She told her husband that if he gave up making designs with the nuts there would be room in their large cave for a great many more and he would soon become the wealthiest chipmunk in the woods. But he would not let her interfere with his designs, so she flew into a rage and left him. "The shrike will get you," she said, "because you are helpless and cannot look after yourself." To be sure, the female chipmunk had not been gone three nights before the male had to dress for a banquet and could not find his studs or shirt or suspenders. So he couldn't go to the banquet, but that was just as well, because all the chipmunks who did go were attacked and killed by a weasel.

The next day the shrike began hanging around outside the chipmunk's cave, waiting to catch him. The shrike couldn't get in because the doorway was clogged up with soiled laundry and dirty dishes. "He will come out for a walk after breakfast and I will get him then," thought the shrike. But the chipmunk slept all day and did not get up and have breakfast until after dark. Then he  came out for a breath of air before beginning work on a new design. The shrike swooped down to snatch up the chipmunk, but could not see very well on account of the dark, so he batted his head against an alder branch and was killed.

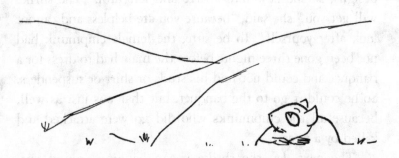

A few days later the female chipmunk returned and saw the awful mess the house was in. She went to the bed and shook her husband. "What would you do without me?" she demanded. "Just go on living, I guess," he said. "You wouldn't last five days," she told him. She swept the house and did the dishes and sent out the laundry, and then she made the chipmunk get up and wash and dress. "You can't be healthy if you lie in bed all day and never get any exercise," she told him. So she took him for a walk in the bright sunlight and they were both caught and killed by the shrike's brother, a shrike named Stoop.

MORAL: *Early to rise and early to bed makes a male healthy and wealthy and dead.*

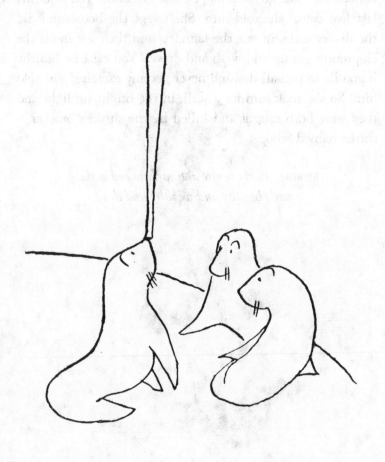

The Seal Who
Became Famous

A SEAL WHO lay basking on a large, smooth rock said to himself: all I ever do is swim. None of the other seals can swim any better than I can, he reflected, but, on the other hand, they can all swim just as well. The more he pondered the monotony and uniformity of his life, the more depressed he became. That night he swam away and joined a circus.

Within two years the seal had become a great balancer. He could balance lamps, billiard cues, medicine balls, hassocks, taborets, dollar cigars, and anything else you gave him. When he read in a book a reference to the Great Seal of the United States, he thought it meant him. In the winter of his third year as a performer he went back to the large, smooth rock to visit his friends and family. He gave them the Big Town stuff right away: the latest slang, liquor in a golden flask, zippers, a gardenia in his lapel. He balanced for them everything there was on the rock to balance, which wasn't much. When he had run through his repertory, he asked the other seals if they could do what he had done and they all said no. "O.K.," he said. "Let's see you do something I can't do." Since the only thing they could do was swim, they all plunged off the rock into the sea.

The circus seal plunged right after them, but he was so hampered by his smart city clothes, including a pair of seventeen-dollar shoes, that he began to founder at once. Since he hadn't been in swimming for three years, he had forgot what to do with his flippers and tail, and he went down for the third time before the other seals could reach him. They gave him a simple but dignified funeral.

MORAL: *Whom God has equipped with flippers*
should not monkey around with zippers.

The Hunter and the Elephant

ONCE UPON A TIME there was a hunter who spent
the best years of his life looking for a pink elephant.
He looked in Cathay and he looked in Africa; he looked in
Zanzibar and he looked in India; but he couldn't find one.

The longer he looked, the more he wanted a pink elephant. He would trample black orchids and he would walk right past purple cows, so intent was he on his quest. Then one day in a far corner of the world he came upon a pink elephant and he spent ten days digging a trap for it and he hired forty natives to help him drive the elephant into the trap. The pink elephant was finally captured and tied up and taken back to America.

When the hunter got home, he found that his farm was really no place for an elephant. It trampled his wife's dahlias and peonies, it broke his children's toys, it crushed the smaller animals around the place, and it smashed pianos and kitchen cabinets as if they were berry boxes. One day, when the hunter had had the elephant for about two years, he woke up to find that his wife had left his bed and his children had left his board and all the animals on the estate were dead except the elephant. The elephant was the same as ever except that it had faded. It wasn't pink any more. It was white.

MORAL: *A burden in the bush is worth two on your hands.*

The Scotty Who Knew Too Much

S EVERAL SUMMERS AGO there was a Scotty who
went to the country for a visit. He decided that all the
farm dogs were cowards, because they were afraid of a certain animal that had a white stripe down its back. "You are

a pussycat and I can lick you," the Scotty said to the farm dog who lived in the house where the Scotty was visiting. "I can lick the little animal with the white stripe, too. Show him to me." "Don't you want to ask any questions about him?" said the farm dog. "Naw," said the Scotty. "*You* ask the questions."

So the farm dog took the Scotty into the woods and showed him the white-striped animal and the Scotty closed in on him, growling and slashing. It was all over in a moment and the Scotty lay on his back. When he came to, the farm dog said, "What happened?" "He threw vitriol," said the Scotty, "but he never laid a glove on me."

A few days later the farm dog told the Scotty there was another animal all the farm dogs were afraid of. "Lead me to him," said the Scotty. "I can lick anything that doesn't wear horseshoes." "Don't you want to ask any questions about him?" said the farm dog. "Naw," said the Scotty. "Just show me where he hangs out." So the farm dog led him to a place in the woods and pointed out the little animal when he came along. "A clown," said the Scotty, "a pushover," and he closed in, leading with his left and exhibiting some mighty fancy footwork. In less than a second the Scotty was flat on his back, and when he woke up the farm dog was pulling quills out of him. "What happened?" said the farm dog. "He pulled a knife on me," said the Scotty, "but at least I have learned how you fight out here in the country, and now I am going to beat *you* up." So he closed in on the farm dog, holding his nose with one front paw to ward off the vitriol and covering his eyes with the other front paw to keep out the knives. The Scotty couldn't see his opponent and he couldn't smell his opponent and he was so badly beaten that he had to be taken back to the city and put in a nursing home.

> MORAL: *It is better to ask some of the questions than to know all the answers.*

The Bear Who Let It Alone

I N THE WOODS of the Far West there once lived a brown bear who could take it or let it alone. He would go into a bar where they sold mead, a fermented drink made of honey, and he would have just two drinks. Then he would put some money on the bar and say, "See what the bears in the back room will have," and he would go home. But finally he took to drinking by himself most of the day. He would reel home at night, kick over the umbrella stand, knock down the bridge lamps, and ram his elbows through the windows. Then he would collapse on the floor and lie there until he went to sleep. His wife was greatly distressed and his children were very frightened.

At length the bear saw the error of his ways and began to reform. In the end he became a famous teetotaller and a persistent temperance lecturer. He would tell everybody that came to his house about the awful effects of drink, and he would boast about how strong and well he had become since he gave up touching the stuff. To demonstrate this, he would stand on his head and on his hands and he would turn cartwheels in the house, kicking over the umbrella stand, knocking down the bridge lamps, and ramming his elbows through the windows. Then he would lie down on the floor, tired by his healthful exercise, and go to sleep. His wife was greatly distressed and his children were very frightened.

MORAL: *You might as well fall flat on your face as lean over too far backward.*

The Owl Who Was God

O NCE UPON A starless midnight there was an owl
who sat on the branch of an oak tree. Two ground
moles tried to slip quietly by, unnoticed. "You!" said the owl.
"Who?" they quavered, in fear and astonishment, for they

could not believe it was possible for anyone to see them in that thick darkness. "You two!" said the owl. The moles hurried away and told the other creatures of the field and forest that the owl was the greatest and wisest of all animals because he could see in the dark and because he could answer any question. "I'll see about that," said a secretary bird, and he called on the owl one night when it was again very dark. "How many claws am I holding up?" said the secretary bird. "Two," said the owl, and that was right. "Can you give me another expression for 'that is to say' or 'namely'?" asked the secretary bird. "To wit," said the owl. "Why does a lover call on his love?" asked the secretary bird. "To woo," said the owl.

The secretary bird hastened back to the other creatures and reported that the owl was indeed the greatest and wisest animal in the world because he could see in the dark and because he could answer any question. "Can he see in the daytime, too?" asked a red fox. "Yes," echoed a dormouse and a French poodle. "Can he see in the daytime, too?" All the other creatures laughed loudly at this silly question, and they set upon the red fox and his friends and drove them out of the region. Then they sent a messenger to the owl and asked him to be their leader.

When the owl appeared among the animals it was high noon and the sun was shining brightly. He walked very slowly, which gave him an appearance of great dignity, and he peered about him with large, staring eyes, which gave him an air of tremendous importance. "He's God!" screamed a Plymouth Rock hen. And the others took up the cry, "He's God!" So they followed him wherever he went and when he began to bump into things they began to bump into things, too. Finally he came to a concrete highway and he started up the middle of it and all the other creatures followed him. Presently a hawk, who was acting as outrider, observed a truck coming toward them at fifty miles an hour, and he reported to the secretary bird and the secretary bird reported to the owl. "There's danger ahead," said the secretary bird. "To wit?" said the owl. The secretary bird told him. "Aren't you afraid?" he asked. "Who?" said the owl calmly, for he could not see the truck. "He's God!" cried all the creatures again, and they were still crying "He's God!" when the truck hit them and ran them down. Some of the animals were merely injured, but most of them, including the owl, were killed.

MORAL: *You can fool too many of the people too much of the time.*

The Sheep in Wolf's Clothing

NOT VERY LONG ago there were two sheep who put on wolf's clothing and went among the wolves as spies, to see what was going on. They arrived on a fete day, when all the wolves were singing in the taverns or dancing in the street. The first sheep said to his companion, "Wolves are just like us, for they gambol and frisk. Every day is fete day in Wolfland." He made some notes on a piece of paper (which a spy should never do) and he headed them "My Twenty-Four Hours in Wolfland," for he had decided not to be a spy any longer but to write a book on Wolfland and also some articles for the *Sheep's Home Companion*. The other sheep guessed what he was planning to do, so he slipped away and began to write a book called "My Ten Hours in Wolfland." The first sheep suspected what was up when he found his friend had gone, so he wired a book to his publisher called "My Five Hours in Wolfland," and it was announced for publication first. The other sheep immediately sold his manuscript to a newspaper syndicate for serialization.

Both sheep gave the same message to their fellows: wolves were just like sheep, for they gambolled and frisked, and every day was fete day in Wolfland. The citizens of Sheepland were convinced by all this, so they drew in their sentinels and they let down their barriers. When the wolves descended on them one night, howling and slavering, the sheep were as easy to kill as flies on a windowpane.

MORAL: *Don't get it right, just get it written.*

The Stork Who Married a Dumb Wife

A DANISH STORK was in the habit of spending six nights a week out on the town with the boys, drinking and dicing and playing the match game. His wife had never left their nest, which was on a chimney top, since

47

he married her, for he did not want her to get wise to the ways of the male. When he got home, which was usually at four o'clock in the morning—unless the party had gone on to Reuben's—he always brought her a box of candy and handed it to her together with a stork story, which is the same as a cock-and-bull story. "I've been out delivering babies," he would say. "It's killing me, but it is my duty to go on." "Who do you deliver babies for?" she asked one morning. "Human beings," he said. "A human being cannot have a baby without help from someone. All the other animals can, but human beings are helpless. They depend on the other animals for everything from food and clothing to companionship." Just then the phone rang and the stork answered it. "Another baby on the way," he said when he had hung up. "I'll have to go out again tonight." So that night he went out again and did not get home until seven-thirty in the morning. "Thish was very special case," he said, handing his wife a box of candy. "Five girls." He did not add that the five girls were all blondes in their twenties.

After a while the female stork got to thinking. Her husband had told her never to leave the nest, because the world was full of stork traps, but she began to doubt this. So she flew out into the world, looking and listening. In this way she learned to tell time and to take male talk with a grain of salt; she found out that candy is dandy, as the poet has said, but that licker is quicker; she discovered that the offspring of the human species are never brought into the world by storks. This last discovery was a great blow to her, but it was a greater blow to Papa when he came home the next morning at a quarter to six. "Hello, you phony obstetrician," said his wife coldly. "How are all the blonde quintuplets today?" And she crowned him with a chimney brick.

MORAL: *The male was made to lie and roam,*
but woman's place is in the home.

The Green Isle
in the Sea

ONE SWEET MORNING in the Year of Our Lord, Nineteen hundred and thirty-nine, a little old gentleman got up and threw wide the windows of his bedroom, letting in the living sun. A black widow spider, who had been dozing on the balcony, slashed at him, and although she missed, she did not miss very far. The old gentleman went downstairs to the dining-room and was just sitting down to a splendid breakfast when his grandson, a boy named Burt, pulled the chair from under him. The old man's hip was strained but it was fortunately not broken.

Out in the street, as he limped toward a little park with many trees, which was to him a green isle in the sea, the old man was tripped up by a gaily-colored hoop sent rolling at him, with a kind of disinterested deliberation, by a grim little girl. Hobbling on a block farther, the old man was startled, but not exactly surprised, when a bold daylight robber stuck a gun in his ribs. "Put 'em up, Mac," said the robber, "and come across." Mac put them up and came across with his watch and money and a gold ring his mother had given him when he was a boy.

When at last the old gentleman staggered into the little park, which had been to him a fountain and a shrine, he saw that half the trees had been killed by a blight, and the other half by a bug. Their leaves were gone and they no longer afforded any protection from the skies, so that the hundred planes which appeared suddenly overhead had an excellent view of the little old gentleman through their bombing-sights.

MORAL: *The world is so full of a number of things, I am sure we should all be as happy as kings, and you know how happy kings are.*

The Crow and the Oriole

ONCE UPON A TIME a crow fell in love with a Baltimore oriole. He had seen her flying past his nest every spring on her way North and every autumn on her way South, and he had decided that she was a tasty dish. He had observed that she came North every year with a different gentleman, but he paid no attention to the fact that all the gentlemen were Baltimore orioles. "Anybody can have that mouse," he said to himself. So he went to his wife and told her that he was in love with a Baltimore oriole who was as cute as a cuff link. He said he wanted a divorce, so his wife gave him one simply by opening the door and handing him his hat. "Don't come crying to me when she throws you down," she said. "That fly-by-season hasn't got a brain in her head. She can't cook or sew. Her upper register sounds like a streetcar taking a curve. You can find out in any dictionary that the crow is the smartest and most capable of birds—or was till you became one." "Tush!" said the male crow. "Pish! You are simply a jealous woman." He tossed her a few dollars. "Here," he said, "go buy yourself some finery. You look like the bottom of an old teakettle." And off he went to look for the oriole.

This was in the springtime and he met her coming North with an oriole he had never seen before. The crow stopped the female oriole and pleaded his cause—or should we say cawed his pleas? At any rate, he courted her in a harsh, grating voice, which made her laugh merrily. "You sound like an old window shutter," she said, and she snapped her fingers at him. "I am bigger and stronger than your gentleman friend," said the crow. "I have a vocabulary larger than his. All the orioles in the country couldn't even lift the corn I own. I am a fine sentinel and my voice can be heard for miles in case of danger." "I don't see how that could interest anybody but another crow," said the female oriole, and she laughed at him and flew on toward the North. The male oriole tossed the crow some coins. "Here," he said, "go buy yourself a blazer or something. You look like the bottom of an old coffeepot."

The crow flew back sadly to his nest, but his wife was not there. He found a note pinned to the front door. "I have gone away with Bert," it read. "You will find some arsenic in the medicine chest."

MORAL: *Even the llama should stick to mamma.*

The Elephant Who
Challenged the World

A N ELEPHANT WHO lived in Africa woke up one
morning with the conviction that he could defeat all
the other animals in the world in single combat, one at a
time. He wondered that he hadn't thought of it before. After
breakfast he called first on the lion. "You are only the King
of Beasts," bellowed the elephant, "whereas I am the Ace!"
and he demonstrated his prowess by knocking the lion out
in fifteen minutes, no holds barred. Then in quick succession
he took on the wild boar, the water buffalo, the rhinoceros,
the hippopotamus, the giraffe, the zebra, the eagle, and the
vulture, and he conquered them all. After that the elephant
spent most of his time in bed eating peanuts, while the other
animals, who were now his slaves, built for him the largest
house any animal in the world had ever had. It was five stories high, solidly made of the hardest woods to be found in
Africa. When it was finished, the Ace of Beasts moved in
and announced that he could pin back the ears of any animal
in the world. He challenged all comers to meet him in the
basement of the big house, where he had set up a prize ring
ten times the regulation size.

Several days went by and then the elephant got an anonymous letter accepting his challenge. "Be in your basement tomorrow afternoon at three o'clock," the message read. So at three o'clock the next day the elephant went down to the basement to meet his mysterious opponent, but there was no one there, or at least no one he could see. "Come out from behind whatever you're behind!" roared the elephant. "I'm not behind anything," said a tiny voice. The elephant tore around the basement, upsetting barrels and boxes, banging his head against the furnace pipes, rocking the house on its foundations, but he could not find his opponent. At the end of an hour the elephant roared that the whole business was a trick and a deceit—probably ventriloquism—and that he would never come down to the basement again. "Oh, yes you will," said the tiny voice. "You will be down here at three o'clock tomorrow and you'll end up on your back." The elephant's laughter shook the house. "We'll see about that," he said.

The next afternoon the elephant, who slept on the fifth floor of the house, woke up at two-thirty o'clock and looked at his wristwatch. "Nobody I can't see will ever get me down to the basement again," he growled, and went back to sleep. At exactly three o'clock the house began to tremble and quiver as if an earthquake had it in its paws. Pillars and beams bent and broke like reeds, for they were all drilled full of tiny holes. The fifth floor gave way completely and crashed down upon the fourth, which fell upon the third, which fell upon the second, which carried away the first as if it had been the floor of a berry basket. The elephant was precipitated into the basement, where he fell heavily upon the concrete floor and lay there on his back, completely unconscious. A tiny voice began to count him out. At the count of ten the elephant came to, but he could not get up. "What animal are you?" he demanded of the mysterious voice in a quavering tone which had lost its menace. "I am the termite," answered the voice.

The other animals, straining and struggling for a week, finally got the elephant lifted out of the basement and put him in jail. He spent the rest of his life there, broken in spirit and back.

MORAL: *The battle is sometimes to the small, for the bigger they are the harder they fall.*

The Birds and the Foxes

ONCE UPON A TIME there was a bird sanctuary in which hundreds of Baltimore orioles lived together happily. The refuge consisted of a forest entirely surrounded by a high wire fence. When it was put up, a pack of foxes who lived nearby protested that it was an arbitrary and unnatural boundary. However, they did nothing about it at the time because they were interested in civilizing the geese and ducks on the neighboring farms. When all the geese and ducks had been civilized, and there was nothing else left to eat, the foxes once more turned their attention to the bird sanctuary. Their leader announced that there had once been foxes in the sanctuary but that they had been driven out. He proclaimed that Baltimore orioles belonged in Baltimore. He said, furthermore, that the orioles in the sanctuary were a continuous menace to the peace of the world. The other animals cautioned the foxes not to disturb the birds in their sanctuary.

So the foxes attacked the sanctuary one night and tore down the fence that surrounded it. The orioles rushed out and were instantly killed and eaten by the foxes.

The next day the leader of the foxes, a fox from whom God was receiving daily guidance, got upon the rostrum and addressed the other foxes. His message was simple and sublime. "You see before you," he said, "another Lincoln. We have liberated all those birds!"

MORAL: *Government of the orioles, by the foxes,*
and for the foxes, must perish from the earth.

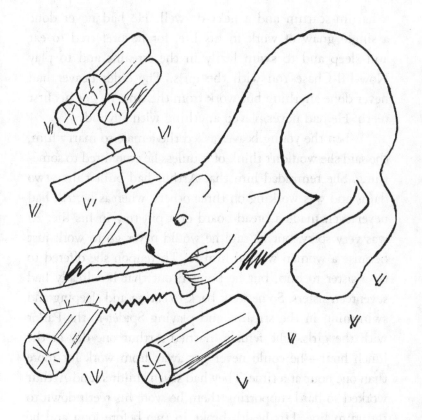

The Courtship of Arthur and Al

ONCE UPON A TIME there was a young beaver named Al and an older beaver named Arthur. They were both in love with a pretty little female. She looked with disfavor upon the young beaver's suit because he was a harum-scarum and a ne'er-do-well. He had never done a single gnaw of work in his life, for he preferred to eat and sleep and to swim lazily in the streams and to play Now-I'll-Chase-You with the girls. The older beaver had never done anything but work from the time he got his first teeth. He had never played anything with anybody.

When the young beaver asked the female to marry him, she said she wouldn't think of it unless he amounted to something. She reminded him that Arthur had built thirty-two dams and was working on three others, whereas he, Al, had never even made a bread-board or a pin tray in his life. Al was very sorry, but he said he would never go to work just because a woman wanted him to. Thereupon she offered to be a sister to him, but he pointed out that he already had seventeen sisters. So he went back to eating and sleeping and swimming in the streams and playing Spider-in-the-Parlor with the girls. The female married Arthur one day at the lunch hour—he could never get away from work for more than one hour at a time. They had seven children and Arthur worked so hard supporting them he wore his teeth down to the gum line. His health broke in two before long and he died without ever having had a vacation in his life. The young beaver continued to eat and sleep and swim in the streams and play Unbutton-Your-Shoe with the girls. He never Got Anywhere, but he had a long life and a Wonderful Time.

MORAL: *It is better to have loafed and lost*
than never to have loafed at all.

The Hen Who Wouldn't Fly

I N ONE OF the Midwestern states there lived a speckled
hen who was opposed to aviation. In her youth, watching
a flight of wild geese going north, she had seen two fall (shot
by hunters), go into a nose dive, and crash into the woods. So

she went about the countryside saying that flying was very dangerous and that any fowl with any sense would stick to the solid earth. Every time she had to cross a concrete highway near her farm she ran on foot, screaming and squawking; sometimes she made it easily, at other times she was almost tagged by passing cars. Five of her sisters and three of her daughters' husbands were killed trying to cross the road in one month (July).

Before long an enterprising wood duck set up an airways service across the road and back. He charged five grains of corn to take a hen or a rooster across, two grains for a chick. But the speckled hen, who was a power in the community, went around clucking and cut-cutting and cadawcutting and telling everybody that air travel was not safe and never would be. She persuaded the chickens not to ride on the duck's back, and he failed in business and returned to the forests. Before the year was out, the speckled hen, four more of her sisters, three of her sons-in-law, four aunts, and a grandfather had been killed trying to cross the road on foot.

MORAL: *Use the wings God gave you, or nothing can save you.*

The Glass in the Field

A SHORT TIME ago some builders, working on a studio in Connecticut, left a huge square of plate glass standing upright in a field one day. A goldfinch flying swiftly across the field struck the glass and was knocked cold. When he came to he hastened to his club, where an attendant bandaged his head and gave him a stiff drink. "What the hell happened?" asked a sea gull. "I was flying across a meadow when all of a sudden the air crystallized on me," said the goldfinch. The sea gull and a hawk and an eagle all laughed heartily. A swallow listened gravely. "For fifteen years, fledgling and bird, I've flown this country," said the eagle, "and I assure you there is no such thing as air crystallizing. Water, yes; air, no." "You were probably struck by a hailstone," the hawk told the goldfinch. "Or he may have had a stroke," said the sea gull. "What do you think, swallow?" "Why, I—I think maybe the air crystallized on him," said the swallow. The large birds laughed so loudly that the goldfinch became annoyed and bet them each a dozen worms that they couldn't follow the course he had flown across the field without encountering the hardened atmosphere. They all took his bet; the swallow went along to watch. The sea gull, the eagle, and the hawk decided to fly together over the route the goldfinch indicated. "You come, too," they said to the swallow. "I—I—well, no," said the swallow. "I don't think I will." So the three large birds took off together and they hit the glass together and they were all knocked cold.

MORAL: *He who hesitates is sometimes saved.*

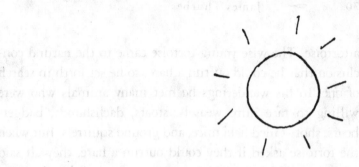

The Tortoise and the Hare

T HERE WAS ONCE a wise young tortoise who read in
an ancient book about a tortoise who had beaten a hare
in a race. He read all the other books he could find but in
none of them was there any record of a hare who had beaten

a tortoise. The wise young tortoise came to the natural conclusion that he could outrun a hare, so he set forth in search
of one. In his wanderings he met many animals who were
willing to race him: weasels, stoats, dachshunds, badger-
boars, short-tailed field mice, and ground squirrels. But when
the tortoise asked if they could outrun a hare, they all said
no, they couldn't (with the exception of a dachshund named
Freddy, and nobody paid any attention to him). "Well, I can,"
said the tortoise, "so there's no use wasting my time on you."
And he continued his search.

After many days, the tortoise finally encountered a hare
and challenged him to a race. "What are you going to use for
legs?" asked the hare. "Never mind that," said the tortoise.
"Read this." He showed the hare the story in the ancient
book, complete with moral about the swift not always being
so terribly fast. "Tosh," said the hare. "You couldn't go fifty
feet in an hour and a half, whereas I can go fifty feet in one
and a fifth seconds." "Posh," said the tortoise. "You probably won't even finish second." "We'll see about that," said
the hare. So they marked off a course fifty feet long. All the
other animals gathered around. A bull-frog set them on their
marks, a gun dog fired a pistol, and they were off.

When the hare crossed the finish line, the tortoise had
gone approximately eight and three-quarter inches.

MORAL: *A new broom may sweep clean,*
but never trust an old saw.

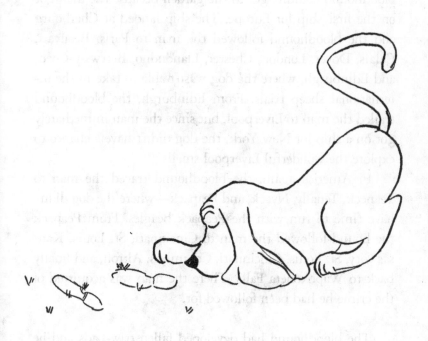

The Patient Bloodhound

I N MAY, 1937, a bloodhound who lived in Wapokoneta
Falls, Ohio, was put on the trail of a man suspected of a
certain crime. The bloodhound followed him to Akron, Cleve-
land, Buffalo, Syracuse, Rochester, Albany, and New York.

The Westminster dog show was going on at the time but the bloodhound couldn't get to the garden because the man got on the first ship for Europe. The ship landed at Cherbourg and the bloodhound followed the man to Paris, Beauvais, Calais, Dover, London, Chester, Llandudno, Bettws-y-Coed, and Edinburgh, where the dog wasn't able to take in the international sheep trials. From Edinburgh, the bloodhound trailed the man to Liverpool, but since the man immediately got on a ship for New York, the dog didn't have a chance to explore the wonderful Liverpool smells.

In America again, the bloodhound traced the man to Teaneck, Tenafly, Nyack, and Peapack—where the dog didn't have time to run with the Peapack beagles. From Peapack the hound followed the man to Cincinnati, St. Louis, Kansas City, St. Louis, Cincinnati, Columbus, Akron, and finally back to Wapokoneta Falls. There the man was acquitted of the crime he had been followed for.

The bloodhound had developed fallen paw-pads and he was so worn out he could never again trail anything that was faster than a turtle. Furthermore, since he had gone through the world with his eyes and nose to the ground, he had missed all its beauty and excitement.

MORAL: *The paths of glory at least lead to the Grave, but the paths of duty may not get you Anywhere.*

The Unicorn in the Garden

ONCE UPON A sunny morning a man who sat in a
breakfast nook looked up from his scrambled eggs to
see a white unicorn with a golden horn quietly cropping the
roses in the garden. The man went up to the bedroom where

his wife was still asleep and woke her. "There's a unicorn in the garden," he said. "Eating roses." She opened one unfriendly eye and looked at him. "The unicorn is a mythical beast," she said, and turned her back on him. The man walked slowly downstairs and out into the garden. The unicorn was still there; he was now browsing among the tulips. "Here, unicorn," said the man, and he pulled up a lily and gave it to him. The unicorn ate it gravely. With a high heart, because there was a unicorn in his garden, the man went upstairs and roused his wife again. "The unicorn," he said, "ate a lily." His wife sat up in bed and looked at him, coldly. "You are a booby," she said, "and I am going to have you put in the booby-hatch." The man, who had never liked the words "booby" and "booby-hatch," and who liked them even less on a shining morning when there was a unicorn in the garden, thought for a moment. "We'll see about that," he said. He walked over to the door. "He has a golden horn in the middle of his forehead," he told her. Then he went back to the garden to watch the unicorn; but the unicorn had gone away. The man sat down among the roses and went to sleep.

As soon as the husband had gone out of the house, the wife got up and dressed as fast as she could. She was very excited and there was a gloat in her eye. She telephoned the police and she telephoned a psychiatrist; she told them to hurry to her house and bring a strait-jacket. When the police and the psychiatrist arrived they sat down in chairs and looked at her, with great interest. "My husband," she said, "saw a unicorn this morning." The police looked at the psychiatrist and the psychiatrist looked at the police. "He told me it ate a lily," she said. The psychiatrist looked at the police and the police looked at the psychiatrist. "He told me it had a golden horn in the middle of its forehead," she said. At a solemn signal from the psychiatrist, the police leaped from their chairs and seized the wife. They had a hard time subduing her, for she put up a terrific struggle, but they finally subdued her. Just as they got her into the strait-jacket, the husband came back into the house.

"Did you tell your wife you saw a unicorn?" asked the police. "Of course not," said the husband. "The unicorn is a mythical beast." "That's all I wanted to know," said the psychiatrist. "Take her away. I'm sorry, sir, but your wife is as crazy as a jay bird." So they took her away, cursing and screaming, and shut her up in an institution. The husband lived happily ever after.

MORAL: *Don't count your boobies until they are hatched.*

The Rabbits Who
Caused All the Trouble

WITHIN THE MEMORY of the youngest child there was a family of rabbits who lived near a pack of wolves. The wolves announced that they did not like the way the rabbits were living. (The wolves were crazy about the way they themselves were living, because it was the only way to live.) One night several wolves were killed in an earthquake and this was blamed on the rabbits, for it is well known that rabbits pound on the ground with their hind legs and cause earthquakes. On another night one of the wolves was killed by a bolt of lightning and this was also blamed on the rabbits, for it is well known that lettuce-eaters cause lightning. The wolves threatened to civilize the rabbits if they didn't behave, and the rabbits decided to run away to a desert island. But the other animals, who lived at a great distance, shamed them, saying, "You must stay where you are and be brave. This is no world for escapists. If the wolves attack you, we will come to your aid, in all probability." So the rabbits continued to live near the wolves and one day there was a terrible flood which drowned a great many wolves. This was blamed on the rabbits, for it is well known that carrot-nibblers with long ears cause floods.

The wolves descended on the rabbits, for their own good, and imprisoned them in a dark cave, for their own protection.

When nothing was heard about the rabbits for some weeks, the other animals demanded to know what had happened to them. The wolves replied that the rabbits had been eaten and since they had been eaten the affair was a purely internal matter. But the other animals warned that they might possibly unite against the wolves unless some reason was given for the destruction of the rabbits. So the wolves gave them one. "They were trying to escape," said the wolves, "and, as you know, this is no world for escapists."

MORAL: *Run, don't walk, to the nearest desert island.*

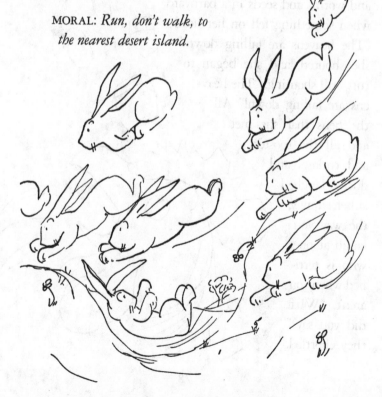

The Hen
and the Heavens

ONCE UPON A TIME a little
red hen was picking up stones
and worms and seeds in a barnyard
when something fell on her head.
"The heavens are falling down!"
she shouted, and she began to
run, still shouting, "The heavens are falling down!" All
the hens that she met
and all the roosters
and turkeys and
ducks laughed
at her, smugly,
the way you
laugh at one
who is terri-
fied when you
aren't. "What
did you say?"
they chortled.

"The heavens are falling down!" cried
the little red hen. Finally a very pompous rooster said to her, "Don't be silly, my
dear, it was only a pea that fell on your
head." And he laughed and laughed
and everybody else except the little
red hen laughed. Then suddenly
with an awful roar great chunks of
crystallized cloud and huge blocks of
icy blue sky began to drop on everybody from above, and everybody was
killed, the laughing rooster and the
little red hen and everybody else in
the barnyard, for the heavens actually
were falling down.

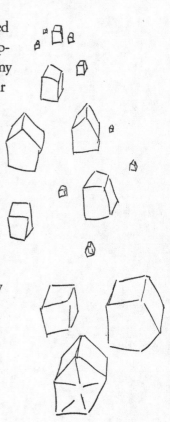

MORAL: *It wouldn't surprise*
me a bit if they did.

Further Fables for Our Time

This book's original dedication read, "To Elmer Davis, whose comprehension of people and persons has lighted our time, so that we can see where we are going, these fables are dedicated with admiration, affection, and thankfulness."

The Sea
and the Shore

A PAIR OF gibbous creatures, who had lived in the sea since time began, which hadn't been long before, were washed upon the shore one day and became the discoverers of land. "The light that never was!" exclaimed the female, lying on the sand in the sun.

"You're always seeing things that never were," grumbled the male. "You're always wanting things that aren't yet."

In the female, lying on the sand in the sun, a dim intuition and prescience began developing. She prefigured mistily things that would one day become rose-point lace and taffeta, sweet perfumes and jewelry. The male, who had a feeling only for wetness and wash, mumbled, "You're a little moist for things like that, a little moist and shapeless."

"I only need to lose a little amorphousness around the waist," she said. "It won't take more than a million years." And she began flobbering, almost imperceptibly, toward the scrubby brown growth beyond the sand and toward the sun. "Come on," she said. But the male had globbed back into the sea, and was gone.

A couple of eons later, the male, unable to get along alone,

reappeared one day upon the shore. He noted with faint satisfaction that the female's shapelessness was beginning to take shape and had become almost shapely. He turned back toward the sea, but a mindless urge deep inside him took on the frail flicker of desire. Suddenly the sea seemed something less than satisfying. He turned about and began flobbering up the sand toward the female, who seemed certain to reach the greening undergrowth in another two thousand years. "Hey, Mag," he shouted. "Wait for baby!"

MORAL: *Let us ponder this basic fact about the human: ahead of every man, not behind him, is a woman.*

The Truth
About Toads

ONE MIDSUMMER NIGHT at the Fauna Club, some of the members fell to boasting, each of his own unique distinction or achievement.

"I am the real Macaw," squawked the Macaw proudly.

"O.K., Mac, take it easy," said the Raven, who was tending bar.

"You should have seen the one I got away from," said the Marlin. "He must have weighed a good two hundred and thirty-five pounds."

"If it weren't for me, the sun would never rise," bragged the Rooster, "and the desire of the night for the morrow would never be gratified." He wiped a tear away. "If it weren't for me, nobody would get up."

"If it weren't for me, there wouldn't *be* anybody," the Stork reminded him proudly.

"I tell them when spring is coming," the Robin chirped.

"I tell them when winter will end," the Groundhog said.

"I tell them how deep the winter will be," said the Woolly Bear.

"I swing low when a storm is coming," said the Spider.

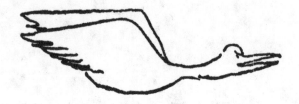

"Otherwise it wouldn't come, and the people would die of a drought."

The Mouse got into the act. "You know where it says, 'Not a creature was stirring, not even a mouse'?" he hiccuped. "Well, gentlemen, that little old mouse was little old me."

"Quiet!" said the Raven, who had been lettering a sign and now hung it prominently above the bar: "Open most hearts and you will see graven upon them Vanity."

The members of the Fauna Club stared at the sign. "Probably means the Wolf, who thinks he founded Rome," said the Cat.

"Or the great Bear, who thinks he is made of stars," said the Mouse.

"Or the golden Eagle, who thinks he's made of gold," said the Rooster.

"Or the Sheep, who thinks men couldn't sleep unless they counted sheep," said the Marlin.

The Toad came up to the bar and ordered a green mint frappé with a firefly in it.

"Fireflies will make you lightheaded," warned the bartender.

"Not me," said the Toad. "Nothing can make me lightheaded. I have a precious jewel in my head." The other members of the club looked at him with mingled disbelief.

"Sure, sure," grinned the bartender, "It's a toadpaz, ain't it, Hoppy?"

"It is an extremely beautiful emerald," said the Toad coldly, removing the firefly from his frappé and swallowing it. "Absolutely priceless emerald. *More* than priceless. Keep 'em comin'."

The bartender mixed another green mint frappé, but he put a slug in it this time instead of a firefly.

"I don't think the Toad has a precious jewel in his head," said the Macaw.

"I do," said the Cat. "Nobody could be that ugly and live unless he had an emerald in his head."

"I'll bet you a hundred fish he hasn't," said the Pelican.

"I'll bet you a hundred clams he has," said the Sandpiper.

The Toad, who was pretty well frappéd by this time, fell asleep, and the members of the club debated how to find out whether his head held an emerald, or some other precious stone. They summoned the Woodpecker from the back room

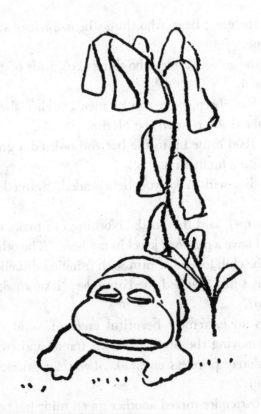

and explained what was up. "If he hasn't got a hole in his head, I'll make one," said the Woodpecker.

There wasn't anything there, gleaming or lovely or precious. The bartender turned out the lights, the Rooster crowed, the sun came up, and the members of the Fauna Club went silently home to bed.

MORAL: *Open most heads and you will find*
nothing shining, not even a mind.

The Butterfly,
the Ladybug,
and the Phoebe

A PHOEBE, A bugwinner for a nestful of fledglings, flew out one day to provide dinner for his family, and came upon a ladybug in frantic flight.

"I know you can catch anything smaller than a golf ball and slower than sound," said the ladybug, "for you are the fastest of the flycatchers, but my house is on fire and my children will burn unless I fly away home."

The phoebe, who had sometimes been guilty of wishing that his own house were on fire, let the ladybug fly away, and turned his attention to a beautiful butterfly.

"Is your house on fire and will your children burn?" the phoebe asked.

"Nothing so mundane as all that," said the butterfly. "I have no children and I have no house, for I am an angel, as anyone can see." She fluttered her wings at the world about her. "This is heaven," she said.

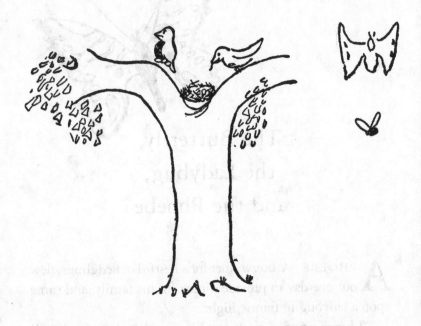

"This is heaven," cried the fledglings, as one fledgling, when they had the butterfly for dessert that night.

MORAL: *She who goes unarmed in Paradise should first be sure that's where she is.*

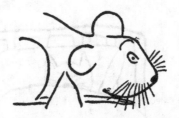

The Foolhardy Mouse
and the Cautious Cat

S UCH SPORT THERE had been that day, in the kitchen
and the pantry, for the cat was away and the mice were
playing all manner of games: mousy-wants-a-corner, hide-
and-squeak, one-old-cat, mouse-in-boots, and so on. Then
the cat came home.

"Cat's back!" whispered Father Mouse.

"Into the wainscoting, all of you!" said Mother Mouse,
and all of the mice except one hastily hid in the woodwork.

The exception was an eccentric mouse named Mervyn,
who had once boldly nipped a bulldog in the ear and got
away with it. Mervyn did not know at the time, and never
found out, that the bulldog was a stuffed bulldog, and so he
lived in a fool's paradise.

The day the cat, whose name was Pouncetta, came back
from wherever she had been, she was astonished to encounter
Mervyn in the butler's pantry, nonchalantly nibbling crumbs.
She crept toward him in her stocking feet and was astounded
when he turned, spit a crumb in her eye, and began insulting
her with a series of insults.

"How did you get out of the bag?" Mervyn inquired calmly. "Put on your pajamas and take a cat nap." He went back to his nibbling, as blasé as you please.

"Steady, Pouncetta," said Pouncetta to herself. "There is more here than meets the eye. This mouse is probably a martyr mouse. He has swallowed poison in the hope that I will eat him and die, so that he can be a hero to a hundred generations of his descendants."

Mervyn looked over his shoulder at the startled and suspicious cat and began to mock her in a mousetto voice. "Doodness dwacious," said Mervyn, "it's a posse cat, in full pursuit of little me." He gestured impudently with one foot. "I went that-a-way," he told Pouncetta. Then he did some other imitations, including a pretty good one of W. C. Fieldmouse.

"Easy, girl," said Pouncetta to herself. "This is a mechanical mouse, a trick mouse with a built-in voice. If I jump on it, it will explode and blow me into a hundred pieces. Damned clever, these mice, but not clever enough for me."

"You'd make wonderful violin strings, if you had any guts," Mervyn said insolently. But Pouncetta did not pounce, in spite of the insult unforgivable. Instead, she turned and stalked out of the butler's pantry and into the sitting room and lay down on her pillow near the fireplace and went to sleep.

When Mervyn got back to his home in the woodwork, his father and mother and brothers and sisters and cousins and uncles and aunts were surprised to see him alive and well. There was great jollity, and the finest cheese was served at a family banquet. "She never laid a paw on me," Mervyn boasted. "I haven't got a scratch. I could take on all the cats in the Catskills." He finished his cheese and went to bed and fell asleep, and dreamed of taking a catamount* in one minute and twenty-eight seconds of the first round.

MORAL: *Fools rush in where angels fear to tread, and the angels are all in Heaven, but few of the fools are dead.*

---

*   A cougar, or any medium-size great cat.

The Rose and the Weed

IN A COUNTRY garden a lovely rose looked down upon a common weed and said, "You are an unwelcome guest, economically useless, and unsightly of appearance. The Devil must love weeds, he made so many of them."

The unwelcome guest looked up at the rose and said, "Lilies that fester smell far worse than weeds, and, one supposes, that goes for roses."

"My name is Dorothy Perkins," the rose said haughtily. "What are you—a beetleweed, a bladderweed, a beggarweed? The names of weeds are ugly." And Dorothy shuddered slightly, but lost none of her pretty petals.

"We have some names prettier than Perkins, or, for my taste, Dorothy, among them silverweed, and jewelweed, and candyweed." The weed straightened a bit and held his ground. "Anywhere you can grow I can grow better," he said.

"I think you must be a burglarweed," said the disdainful Miss Perkins, "for you get in where you aren't wanted, and take what isn't yours—the rain and the sunlight and the good earth."

The weed smiled a weedy smile. "At least," he said, "I do not come from a family of climbers."

The rose drew herself up to her full height. "I'd have you know that roses are the emblem of old England," she said. "We are the flower of song and story."

"And of war," the weed replied. "The summer winds take you by storm, not you the winds with beauty. I've seen it happen many times, to roses of yesteryear, long gone and long forgotten."

"We are mentioned in Shakespeare," said the rose, "many times in many plays. The lines are too sweet for your ears, but I will tell you some."

Just then, and before Miss Perkins could recite, a wind came out of the west, riding low to the ground and swift, like the cavalry of March, and Dorothy Perkins' beautiful disdain suddenly became a scattering of petals, economically useless, and of appearance not especially sightly. The weed stood firm, his head to the wind, armored, or so he thought, in security and strength, but as he was brushing a few rose

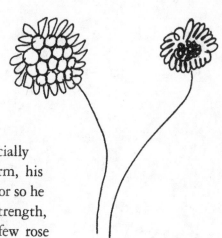

petals and aphids from his lapels, the hand of the gardener flashed out of the air and pulled him out of the ground by the roots before you could say Dorothy Perkins, or, for that matter, jewelweed.

> MORAL: *Tout, as the French say, in a philosophy older than ours and an idiom often more succinct, passe.*

The Bat Who
Got the Hell Out

A COLONY OF bats living in a great American cave
had got along fine for a thousand generations, flying,
hanging head down, eating insects, and raising young, and
then one year a male named Flitter, who had fluttered se-
cretly out of his room at night and flown among the haunts
of men, told his father that he had decided to get the hell
out. The shocked father sent Flitter to Fleder, the great-great-
grandfather of all the bats in the cave.

"You should be proud of being a bat among bats," said
old Fleder, "for we are one of the oldest species on the planet,
much older than Man, and the only mammal capable of true
flight."

The discontented young bat was not impressed. "I want
to live like a man among men," he said. "Men have the best
food, and the most fun, and the cutest females."

At this, old Fleder stormed about the cave, squeaking
unintelligibly. Then he recovered his calm and continued his
talk. "A man got into my room one night," he said, "and
managed somehow to tangle me in his hair. It was a shattering experience, from which I shall never completely recover."

"When men die they go to Heaven, but when bats are dead they are dead," said Flitter. "I want to go to Heaven when I die."

This amused old Fleder in a gaunt and gloomy sort of way, and he chittered, quickered, and zickered for some moments before he could say, "You have no more soul than a moose, or a mouse, or a mole. You should be glad that you will never become an angel, for angels do not have true flight. One wants to *sleep* through eternity, not bumble and flap about forever like a bee or a butterfly."

But Flitter had made up his mind, and the old bat's words of wisdom were in vain. That night, the discontented young bat quit the bat colony, and flickered out of the cave, in the confident hope of giving up his membership in the Chiroptera and joining the happy breed of men. Unfortunately for his dream, he spent his first night hanging head down from the rafters of an auditorium in which a best-selling Inspirationalist was dragging God down to the people's level. Ushers moved silently among the rapt listeners, selling copies of the speaker's books: *Shake Hands with the Almighty*, *You Can Be Jehovah's Pal*, and *Have You Taken Out Eternity Insurance?* The speaker was saying, "Have a little talk with the Lord while you're waiting for a bus, or riding to work, or sitting in the dentist's chair. Have comfy chats with the Lord in the little cozy corners of spare time."

Flitter decided that there was something the matter with the acoustics, or with his tragus, caused by hanging head down in the presence of the Eternal Species, but when he began flying about the auditorium, there was no change in the nature of the English sentences. "Tell the Lord to put it there," the inspired man went on. "Give him your duke." The speaker waved clasped hands above his head and gazed up at the ceiling. "Keep pitching, God," he said. "You've got two strikes on Satan."

Flitter, who had never felt sick before in his life, felt sick, and decided to get the air. After he had got the air, he realized that he did not want to become a member of the species *Homo sapiens*, because of the danger of bumbling or flapping into the Inspirationalist after they had both become angels. And so Flitter returned to the cave, and everybody was astonished to see him, and nobody said anything, and for a time there was a great silence.

"I've come the hell back," said Flitter, meekly. And he resumed, without discontent, the immemorial life of the Chiroptera,* flying, hanging head down, eating insects, and raising young.

MORAL: *By decent minds is he abhorred*
who'd make a Babbitt† of the Lord.

---

*   The mammalian Order that includes bats.
†   Based on the character in Sinclair Lewis's novel *Babbitt*, the word has come to mean a smug, complacent, middle-class person.

The Lion and the Foxes

THE LION HAD just explained to the cow, the goat,
and the sheep that the stag they had killed belonged
to him, when three little foxes appeared on the scene.

"I will take a third of the stag as a penalty," said one, "for you have no hunter's license."

"I will take a third of the stag for your widow," said another, "for that is the law."

"I have no widow," said the lion.

"Let us not split hairs," said the third fox, and he took his share of the stag as a withholding tax. "Against a year of famine," he explained.

"But I am king of beasts," roared the lion.

"Ah, then you will not need the antlers, for you have a crown," said the foxes, and they took the antlers, too.

MORAL: *It is not as easy to get the lion's share nowadays as it used to be.*

The Wolf
Who Went Places

A WEALTHY YOUNG wolf, who was oblivious of everything except himself, was tossed out of college for cutting classes and corners, and he decided to see if he could travel around the world in eighty minutes.

"That isn't possible," his grandmother told him, but he only grinned at her.

"The impossible is the most fun," he said.

She went with him to the door of the old Wolf place. "If you go that fast, you won't live to regret it," she warned him, but he grinned again, showing a tongue as long as a necktie.

"That's an old wolves' tale," he said, and went on his reckless way.

He bought a 1959 Blitzen Bearcat, a combination motorcar and airplane, with skyrocket getaway, cyclone speedrive, cannonball takeoff, blindall headlights, magical retractable monowings, and lightning pushbutton transformationizer. "How fast can this crate go without burning up?" he asked the Blitzen Bearcat salesman.

"I don't know," the salesman said, "but I have a feeling you'll find out."

The wealthy young wolf smashed all the ground records and air records and a lot of other things in his trip around the world, which took him only 78.5 minutes from the time he knocked down the Washington Monument on his takeoff to the time he landed where it had stood. In the crowd that welcomed him home, consisting of about eleven creatures, for all the others were hiding under beds, there was a speed-crazy young wolfess, with built-in instantaneous pickup ability, and in no time at all the wolf and his new-found mate were setting new records for driving upside down, backward, blindfolded, handcuffed, and cockeyed, doubled and redoubled.

One day, they decided to see if they could turn in to Central Park from Fifth Avenue while traveling at a rate of 175 miles an hour, watching television, and holding hands. There was a tremendous shattering, crashing, splitting, roaring, blazing, cracking, and smashing, ending in a fiery display of wheels, stars, cornices, roofs, treetops, glass, steel, and people, and it seemed to those spectators who did not die of seizures as they watched that great red portals opened in the sky, swinging inward on mighty hinges, revealing an endless nowhere, and then closed behind the flying and flaming wolves with a clanking to end all clanking, as if those gates which we have been assured shall not prevail had, in fact, prevailed.

MORAL: *Where most of us end up there is no knowing, but the hellbent get where they are going.*

The Bluebird
and His Brother

I T WAS SAID of two bluebirds that they were unlike as two brothers could be, that one was a pearl in a pod and the other a pea. Pearl was happy-go-lucky, and Pea was gloomy-go-sorry.

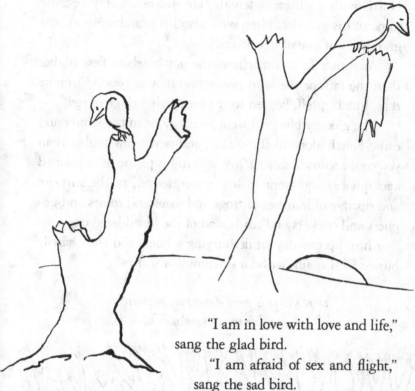

"I am in love with love and life,"
sang the glad bird.

"I am afraid of sex and flight,"
sang the sad bird.

Pearl flaunted his gay colors like a bonnie blue flag, and his song was as bold as the rebel yell. He went South every winter alone, and came North every spring with a different female. His gay philosophy freed his psyche of the stains of fear and the stresses of guilt, and he attained a serenity of spirit that few male birds and even fewer male human beings ever reach. He did not worry because some of his children were also his nieces, the daughters of one of his sisters. He sat loose, sang pretty, and slept tight, in a hundred honey locusts and cherry trees and lilac bushes. And every winter he went South alone, and every spring he came

North with a different female. He did not worry because some of his grandchildren were also his grandnephews, the grandsons of one of his sisters.

At sunset in summertime, the gay bluebird flew higher than the lark or the wild goose, and he was pleased to note that, like himself, heaven wore blue, with a tinge of red.

The gloomy bluebird went South alone in the winter and came North alone in the spring, and never flew higher than you could throw a sofa. While still in his prime he developed agoraphobia and went to live underground, to the surprise and dismay of families of frogs and foxes and moles and gophers and crickets and toads, and of the bewildered dog who dug him up one day while burying a bone, and then hastily buried him again, without ceremony or sorrow.

MORAL: *It is more dangerous to straight-arm life than to embrace it.*

The Clothes Moth
and the Luna Moth

A CLOTHES MOTH who lived in a closet and had never done anything, or wanted to do anything, except eat wool and fur, flew out of his closet one twilight just in time to see a lovely Luna moth appear on the outside of a window-pane. The Luna moth fluttered against the lighted glass as gracefully as a drifting autumn leaf, and she was dressed in a charming evening gown. What interested her was the flame of a candle burning in the room, burning on the mantelpiece above the fireplace, but the clothes moth thought she was making signs at him, and he conceived a great desire for her.

"I have to have you," said the clothes moth, but the Luna moth laughed, and her laughter was like the bells of elfland faintly tinkling.

"Go eat a shroud," said the Luna moth haughtily. "You are as vulgar as a tent moth, or a gypsy moth, and nowhere near as handsome as a tiger moth."

"If you come to live with me I will feed you on sweaters and stoles," said the clothes moth, whose ardor was only increased by the lovely Luna's scorn.

"You are a flug, who can flugger, but not fly or flutter,"

said the Luna moth, trying to get through the windowpane and reach the star on the mantelpiece.

"You can have wedding dresses and evening clothes and a mink coat," panted the clothes moth, and again the Luna moth's laughter was like the bells of elfland faintly tinkling.

"I live on twilight and the stars," she said.

"It was love at first flight," the clothes moth protested. "It was love at first flutter."

The Luna moth's tiny silvery tone became sharper. "You are a mulch," she said, "a mulbus, a crawg, and a common creeb."

All these words were words a nice moth rarely uses, but they had no effect upon the passion of the clothes moth.

"I know you have one wing in the grave," he told her. "I know you're not long for this world, and so I must have you as soon as I can. A thing of beauty is a joy for such a little time."

The lovely Luna moth tried to cajole her admirer into opening the window—so that she could fly to the fascinating flame above the fireplace, but she did not tell him this. She let him believe that his drab gray lovemaking had won her heart. In his desire to reach her, he flew against the windowpane time and time again, and finally made a small opening in it, and  then fluggered crazily to the floor, dead of a broken head and wings and body. The lovely Luna, whose desire for the star is a matter of immortal record, flew swiftly and gracefully toward the candle on the mantelpiece and was consumed in its flame with a little zishing sound like that made by a lighted cigarette dropped in a cup of coffee.

MORAL: *Love is blind, but desire just doesn't give a good goddamn.*

The Lover
and His Lass

AN ARROGANT GRAY parrot
and his arrogant mate listened,
one African afternoon, in disdain and
derision, to the lovemaking of a lover and
his lass, who happened to be hippopotamuses.

"He calls her snooky-ookums," said Mrs.
Gray. "Can you believe that?"

"No," said Gray. "I don't see how any male
in his right mind could entertain affection for a
female that has no more charm than a capsized
bathtub."

"Capsized bathtub, indeed!" exclaimed Mrs. Gray. "Both of them have the appeal of a coastwise fruit steamer with a cargo of waterlogged basketballs."

But it was spring, and the lover and his lass were young, and they were oblivious of the scornful comments of their sharp-tongued neighbors, and they continued to bump each other around in the water, happily pushing and pulling, backing and filling, and snorting and snaffling. The tender things they said to each other during the monolithic give-and-take of their courtship sounded as lyric to them as flowers in bud or green things opening. To the Grays, however, the bumbling romp of the lover and his lass was hard to comprehend and even harder to tolerate, and for a time they thought of calling the A.B.I., or African Bureau of Investigation, on the ground that monolithic lovemaking by enormous creatures who should have become decent fossils long ago was probably a threat to the security of the jungle. But they decided instead to phone their friends and neighbors and gossip about the shameless pair, and describe them in mocking and monstrous metaphors involving skidding buses on icy streets and overturned moving vans.

Late that evening, the hippopotamus and the hippopotama were surprised and shocked to hear the Grays exchanging terms of endearment. "Listen to those squawks," wuffled the male hippopotamus.

"What in the world can they see in each other?" gurbled the female hippopotamus.

"I would as soon live with a pair of unoiled garden shears," said her inamoratus.

They called up their friends and neighbors and discussed the incredible fact that a male gray parrot and a female gray

parrot could possibly have any sex appeal. It was long after midnight before the hippopotamuses stopped criticizing the Grays and fell asleep, and the Grays stopped maligning the hippopotamuses and retired to their beds.

MORAL: *Laugh and the world laughs with you, love and you love alone.*

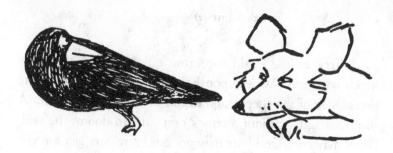

The Fox
and the Crow

A CROW, PERCHED in a tree with a piece of cheese in his beak, attracted the eye and nose of a fox. "If you can sing as prettily as you sit," said the fox, "then you are the prettiest singer within my scent and sight." The fox had read somewhere, and somewhere, and somewhere else, that praising the voice of a crow with a cheese in his beak would make him drop the cheese and sing. But this is not what happened to this particular crow in this particular case.

"They say you are sly and they say you are crazy," said the crow, having carefully removed the cheese from his beak with the claws of one foot, "but you must be nearsighted as well. Warblers wear gay hats and colored jackets and bright vests, and they are a dollar a hundred. I wear black and I am unique." He began nibbling the cheese, dropping not a single crumb.

"I am sure you are," said the fox, who was neither crazy nor nearsighted, but sly. "I recognize you, now that I look more closely, as the most famed and talented of all birds, and I fain would hear you tell about yourself, but I am hungry and must go."

"Tarry awhile," said the crow quickly, "and share my lunch with me." Whereupon he tossed the cunning fox the lion's share of the cheese, and began to tell about himself. "A ship that sails without a crow's nest sails to doom," he said. "Bars may come and bars may go, but crow bars last forever. I am the pioneer of flight, I am the map maker. Last, but never least, my flight is known to scientists and engineers, geometrists and scholars, as the shortest distance between two points. Any two points," he concluded arrogantly.

"Oh, every two points, I am sure," said the fox. "And thank you for the lion's share of what I know you could not spare." And with this he trotted away into the woods, his appetite appeased, leaving the hungry crow perched forlornly in the tree.

MORAL: *'Twas true in Aesop's time, and La Fontaine's, and now, no one else can praise thee quite so well as thou.*

Variations on the Theme

I

A fox, attracted by the scent of something, followed his nose to a tree in which sat a crow with a piece of cheese in his beak. "Oh, cheese," said the fox scornfully. "That's for mice."

The crow removed the cheese with his talons and said, "You always hate the thing you cannot have, as, for instance, grapes."

"Grapes are for the birds," said the fox haughtily. "I am an epicure, a gourmet, and a gastronome."

The embarrassed crow, ashamed to be seen eating mouse food by a great specialist in the art of dining, hastily dropped the cheese. The fox caught it deftly, swallowed it with relish, said *"Merci,"* politely, and trotted away.

II

A fox had used all his blandishments in vain, for he could not flatter the crow in the tree and make him drop the cheese he held in his beak. Suddenly, the crow tossed the cheese to the astonished fox. Just then the farmer, from whose kitchen the loot had been stolen, appeared, carrying a rifle, looking for the robber. The fox turned and ran for the woods. "There goes the guilty son of a vixen now!" cried the crow, who, in case you do not happen to know it, can see the glint of sunlight on a gun barrel at a greater distance than anybody.

III

This time the fox, who was determined not to be outfoxed by a crow, stood his ground and did not run when the farmer appeared, carrying a rifle and looking for the robber.

"The teeth marks in this cheese are mine," said the fox, "but the beak marks were made by the true culprit up there in the tree. I submit this cheese in evidence, as Exhibit A, and bid you and the criminal a very good day." Whereupon he lit a cigarette and strolled away.

IV

In the great and ancient tradition, the crow in the tree with the cheese in his beak began singing, and the cheese fell into the fox's lap. "You sing like a shovel," said the fox, with a grin, but the crow pretended not to hear and cried out, "Quick, give me back the cheese! Here comes the farmer with his rifle!"

"Why should I give you back the cheese?" the wily fox demanded.

"Because the farmer has a gun, and I can fly faster than you can run."

So the frightened fox tossed the cheese back to the crow, who ate it, and said, "Dearie me, my eyes are playing tricks on me—or am I playing tricks on you? Which do you think?" But there was no reply, for the fox had slunk away into the woods.

The Bears
and the Monkeys

I N A DEEP forest there lived many bears. They spent the winter sleeping, and the summer playing leap-bear and stealing honey and buns from nearby cottages. One day a fast-talking monkey named Glib showed up and told them that their way of life was bad for bears. "You are prisoners of pastime," he said, "addicted to leap-bear, and slaves of honey and buns."

The bears were impressed and frightened as Glib went on talking. "Your forebears have done this to you," he said. Glib was so glib, glibber than the glibbest monkey they had ever seen before, that the bears believed he must know more than they knew, or than anybody else. But when he left, to tell other species what was the matter with *them*, the bears reverted to their fun and games and their theft of buns and honey.

Their decadence made them bright of eye, light of heart, and quick of paw, and they had a wonderful time, living as bears had always lived, until one day two of Glib's successors appeared, named Monkey Say and Monkey Do. They were even glibber than Glib, and they brought many presents and

smiled all the time. "We have come to liberate you from freedom," they said. "This is the New Liberation, twice as good as the old, since there are two of us."

So each bear was made to wear a collar, and the collars were linked together with chains, and Monkey Do put a ring in the lead bear's nose, and a chain on the lead bear's ring. "Now you are free to do what I tell you to do," said Monkey Do.

"Now you are free to say what I want you to say," said Monkey Say. "By sparing you the burden of electing your leaders, we save you from the dangers of choice. No more secret ballots, everything open and aboveboard."

For a long time the bears submitted to the New Liberation, and chanted the slogan the monkeys had taught them: "Why stand on your own two feet when you can stand on ours?"

Then one day they broke the chains of their new freedom and found their way back to the deep forest and began

playing leap-bear again and stealing honey and buns from the nearby cottages. And their laughter and gaiety rang through the forest, and birds that had ceased singing began singing again, and all the sounds of the earth were like music.

MORAL: *It is better to have the ring of freedom in your ears than in your nose.*

The Father
and His Daughter

A LITTLE GIRL was given so many picture books on her seventh birthday that her father, who should have run his office and let her mother run the home, thought his daughter should give one or two of her new books to a little neighbor boy named Robert, who had dropped in, more by design than by chance.

Now, taking books, or anything else, from a little girl is like taking arms from an Arab, or candy from a baby, but the father of the little girl had his way and Robert got two of her books. "After all, that leaves you with nine," said the father, who thought he was a philosopher and a child psychologist, and couldn't shut his big fatuous mouth on the subject.

A few weeks later, the father went to his library to look up "father" in the Oxford English Dictionary, to feast his eyes on the praise of fatherhood through the centuries, but he couldn't find volume F–G, and then he discovered that three others were missing, too—A–B, L–M, and V–Z. He began a probe of his household, and soon learned what had become of the four missing volumes.

"A man came to the door this morning," said his little daughter, "and he didn't know how to get from here to Torrington, or from Torrington to Winsted, and he was a nice man, much nicer than Robert, and so I gave him four of your books. After all, there are thirteen volumes in the Oxford English Dictionary, and that leaves you nine."

MORAL: *This truth has been known from here to Menander*: what's sauce for the gosling's not sauce for the gander.*

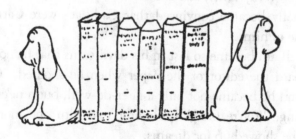

---

*   A comic dramatist of ancient Greece.

The Cat
in the Lifeboat

A FELINE NAMED William got a job as copy cat on a
daily paper and was surprised to learn that every other
cat on the paper was named Tom, Dick, or Harry. He soon
found out that he was the only cat named William in town.
The fact of his singularity went to his head, and he began
confusing it with distinction. It got so that whenever he saw
or heard the name William, he thought it referred to him.
His fantasies grew wilder and wilder, and he came to believe
that he was the Will of Last Will and Testament, and the
Willy of Willy Nilly, and the cat who put the cat in catnip.
He finally became convinced that Cadillacs were Catillacs
because of him.

William became so lost in his daydreams that he no longer heard the editor of the paper when he shouted, "Copy
cat!" and he became not only a ne'er-do-well, but a ne'er-do-
anything. "You're fired," the editor told him one morning
when he showed up for dreams.

"God will provide," said William jauntily.

"God has his eye on the sparrow," said the editor.

"So've I," said William smugly.

William went to live with a cat-crazy woman who had nineteen other cats, but they could not stand William's egotism or the tall tales of his mythical exploits, honors, blue ribbons, silver cups, and medals, and so they all left the woman's house and went to live happily in huts and hovels. The cat-crazy woman changed her will and made William her sole heir, which seemed only natural to him, since he believed that all wills were drawn in his favor. "I am eight feet tall," William told her one day, and she smiled and said, "I should say you are, and I am going to take you on a trip around the world and show you off to everybody."

William and his mistress sailed one bitter March day on the S.S. *Forlorna*, which ran into heavy weather, high seas, and hurricane. At midnight the cargo shifted in the towering seas, the ship listed menacingly, SOS calls were frantically sent out, rockets were fired into the sky, and the officers began running up and down companionways and corridors shouting, "Abandon ship!" And then another shout arose, which seemed only natural to the egotistical cat. It was, his vain ears told him, the loud repetition of "William and children first!" Since William figured no lifeboat would be launched until he was safe and sound, he dressed leisurely, putting on white tie and tails, and then sauntered out on deck. He leaped lightly into a lifeboat that was being lowered, and found himself in the company of a little boy named Johnny Green and another little boy named Tommy Trout, and their mothers, and other children and their mothers. "Toss that cat overboard!" cried the sailor in charge of the lifeboat, and Johnny Green threw him overboard, but Tommy Trout pulled him back in.

"Let *me* have that tomcat," said the sailor, and he took William in his big right hand and threw him, like a long incompleted forward pass, about forty yards from the tossing lifeboat.

When William came to in the icy water, he had gone down for the twenty-fourth time, and had thus lost eight of his lives, so he only had one left. With his remaining life and strength he swam and swam until at last he reached the sullen shore of a sombre island inhabited by surly tigers, lions, and other great cats. As William lay drenched and panting on the shore, a jaguar and a lynx walked up to him and asked him who he was and where he came from. Alas, William's dreadful experience in the lifeboat and the sea had produced traumatic amnesia, and he could not remember who he was or where he came from.

"We'll call him Nobody," said the jaguar.

"Nobody from Nowhere," said the lynx.

And so William lived among the great cats on the island until he lost his ninth life in a barroom brawl with a young panther who had asked him what his name was and where he came from and got what he considered an uncivil answer.

The great cats buried William in an unmarked grave because, as the jaguar said, "What's the good of putting up a stone reading 'Here lies Nobody from Nowhere'?"

MORAL: *O why should the spirit of mortal be proud,*
in this little voyage from swaddle to shroud?

The Bragdowdy
and the Busybody

A FEMALE HARE, who had been born with a foot in everybody's affairs, became known in her community as "that big Belgian busybody." She was always listening to the thumpings of her neighbors. "You're all ears," her mate snarled one day. "For God's sake, get some *laissez faire*." There was no answer, for she had hopped next door to exhort, reproach, and upbraid a female guinea pig who had borne one hundred and seventy-three young and had then let herself go. She had become a bragdowdy, and spent her time weeping over *True Pigtales*.

"Where is your civic spirit?" demanded Mrs. Hare. "And your country, state, federal, and global spirit? Look at me. I am president, or chairwoman, of practically everything, and founder of the Listening Post, an organization of eight hundred females with their ears to the ground."

The male guinea pig, who had been lying on a lettuce leaf, taking it easy, tried to hide from his nosy neighbor, but she came into the room, buttocky buttocky, before he could get out of bed.

"A big strapping male like you," she scoffed, "lying around

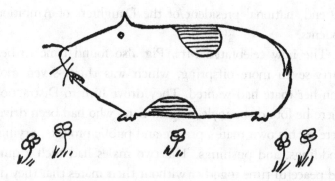

the house when you ought to be at the laboratory, having injections to see whether some new serum is deadly or not." The male guinea pig's teeth began to chatter, and when a male guinea pig's teeth chatter it doesn't mean he's afraid, it means he's mad. But the Belgian busybody didn't care how anybody felt except herself. "You and your mate should join things and do things!" she exclaimed. "Shoulder to the wheel, nose to the grindstone, best foot forward, finger in the pie, knee on the chest!"

Before many weeks had passed, Mrs. Pig developed a guilt complex that manifested itself in an activity compulsion. She gave up reading *True Pigtales*, took her mate's edible bed away from him, straightened up the house, and joined twenty-four up-and-coming organizations. She became famous for keeping everybody on his toes, whether that's where he wanted to be or not. She was made chairman of the Bear a Basket of Babies Committee, secretary of the Get Behind Your Mate and Push Movement, treasurer of the Don't Let Dad Dawdle League, inventor of its slogan, "He can do twice as much in half the time if he puts your mind to it," and, in the end, national president of the Daughters of Ambitious Rodents.

The now celebrated Mrs. Pig also found time to bear thirty-seven more offspring, which was thirty-seven more than her mate had wanted. They drove him to Distraction, where he found the male Belgian hare, who had been driven there by his own mate's private and public projects, pryings, proddings, and pushings. The two males had such a quiet and peaceful time together without their mates that they decided to keep it that way. Representatives of ninety-six different organizations—the seventy-two Mrs. Hare belonged to and Mrs. Pig's twenty-four—argued with them in vain. They ran away one night while their mates were addressing the He Could If He Wanted To, He's Just Not Trying Club,

without so much as a fare-thee-well or a note on a pillow, and leaving no forwarding address. They decided to go to Tahiti to forget, but long before they reached Tahiti they had forgot.

MORAL: *Thou shalt not convert thy neighbor's wife, nor yet louse up thy neighbor's life.*

The Human Being
and the Dinosaur

A GES AGO in a wasteland of time and a wilderness of space, Man, in upper case, and dinosaur, in lower, first came face to face. They stood like stones for a long while, wary and watchful, taking each other in. Something told the dinosaur that he beheld before him the coming glory and terror of the world, and in the still air of the young planet he seemed to catch the faint smell of his own inevitable doom.

"Greetings, stupid," said Man. "Behold in me the artfully articulated architect of the future, the chosen species, the certain survivor, the indestructible one, the monarch of all you survey, and of all that everyone else surveys, for that matter. On the other hand, you are, curiously enough, for all your size, a member of the inconsequent ephemera. You are one of God's moderately amusing early experiments, a frail footnote to natural history, a contraption in a museum for future Man to marvel at, an excellent example of Jehovah's jejune juvenilia."

The dinosaur sighed with a sound like thunder.

"Perpetuating your species," Man continued, "would be foolish and futile."

132

"The missing link is not lost," said the dinosaur sorrowfully. "It's hiding."

Man paid the doomed dinosaur no mind. "If there were no Man it would be necessary to create one," said Man, "for God moves in mysterious, but inefficient, ways, and He needs help. Man will go on forever, but you will be one with the mammoth and the mastodon, for monstrosity is the behemother of extinction."

"There are worse things than being extinct," said the dinosaur sourly, "and one of them is being you."

Man strutted a little pace and flexed his muscles. "You cannot even commit murder," he said, "for murder requires a mind. You are capable only of dinosaurslaughter. You and your ilk are incapable of devising increasingly effective methods of destroying your own species and, at the same time, increasingly miraculous methods of keeping it extant. You will never live to know the two-party system, the multi-party system, and the one-party system. You will be gone long before I have made this the best of all possible worlds, no matter how possible all other worlds may be. In your highest state of evolution you could not develop the brain cells to prove innocent men guilty, even after their acquittal. You are all wrong in the crotch, and in the cranium, and in the cortex. But I have wasted enough time on you. I must use these fingers which God gave me, and now probably wishes He had kept for Himself, to begin writing those noble volumes about Me which will one day run to several hundred billion items, many of them about war, death, conquest, decline, fall, blood, sweat, tears, threats, warnings, boasts, hopelessness, hell, heels, and whores. There will be little enough about you and your ilk and your kith and your kin, for after all, who were you and your ilk and your kith and your kin? Good day and goodbye," said Man in conclusion. "I shall see to it that your species receives a decent burial, with some simple ceremony."

Man, as it turned out, was right. The dinosaur and his ilk and his kith and his kin died not long after, still in lower case, but with a curious smile of satisfaction, or something of the sort, on their ephemeral faces.

MORAL: *The noblest study of mankind is Man, says Man.*

The Hen Party

ALL THE HENS came to Lady Buff Orpington's tea party and, as usual, Minnie Minorca was the last to arrive, for, as usual, she had spent the day with her psychiatrist, her internist, and her beak, comb, and gizzard specialist. "I'm not long for this barnyard," she told the other hens. "What do you suppose I've got *now?*" She went about the room, giving all the hens a peck except her hostess, who pecked her, but without affection.

"I've got blue comb," Minnie went on.

A chill had fallen upon the gathering, as it always did when Minnie Minorca began reciting her complaints, old and new, real and hysterical. "Dr. Leghorn found out today that I am edentulous, and he told me so," said Minnie, triumphantly. "Of course I've always had chronic coryza, Newcastle disease, and laryngotracheitis."

"Minnie has so many pains she has given each of us one," said Lady Buff Orpington coldly. "Isn't that nice?"

"I love you girls," said Minnie, "and I love to share my troubles with you. You're such good listeners. I was telling my psychiatrist about my new ailments, including incipient dry feather, and he suddenly blurted out some of the things

135

he has been keeping from me all these years. He said I have galloping aggression, inflamed ego, and too much gall."

"Now there's a psychiatrist who knows what he's talking about," said Miss Brahma, and she tried to talk to her hostess about the weather, and the other hens tried to talk to one another, but Minnie Minorca kept on telling how charged with punishments her scroll was. As she rambled on, describing in detail the attack of scale foot she had had in Cadawcutt, Connecticut, one of the hens whispered, "I've just put some sleeping pills in her teacup."

"You must have some more tea," cried Lady Buff Orpington, as she refilled Minnie's cup, and all her guests repeated,

"You must have some more tea," and Minnie Minorca, delighted to be the center of attention and, as she thought, concern, hastily drank the slugged tea. After she had passed out, one of the hens suggested that they wring her neck while the wringing was good. "We could say she broke her neck trying to see what was the matter with her tail," the conspirator suggested.

Lady Buff Orpington sighed and said, "We'll draw lots to see who wrings her neck at the next tea party someone gives. Now let's go out and take a dust bath and leave old Fuss and Fevers to her nightmares." And the hostess and her guests went out into the road, leaving Minnie Minorca to dream of a brand-new ailment, called Minnieitis, or Mrs. Minorca's disease.

MORAL: *Misery's love of company oft goeth unrequited.*

The Rose, the Fountain,
and the Dove

IN A GREEN valley, serene as a star and silent as the moon—except for the Saturday laughter of children and the sound of summer thunder—a rose and a fountain grew restless as time crept on.

"This is our sorrow: we're here today and here tomorrow," sighed the rose. "I wish I were rootloose and fancy-free, like the dove."

"I want to see what's in the wood," the fountain said. "I want to have adventures to cherish and regret." He signalled the dove in a cipher of sparkle, and the dove came down from the sky and made a graceful landing.

"What's in the wood?" the fountain asked. "You have wings and you must know, for there's nowhere you cannot go."

"I like to fly above the green valley," said the dove. "The green valley is all I know, and all I want to know."

"Stars fall in a pool in the wood," the rose declared. "I hear them sputter when they strike the water. I could fish them up and dry them out and sell them to a king, if I had wings like you," she told the dove.

"I like it where I am," the dove replied, "flying above the valley. I watch the stars that do not fall, and would not want to sell them."

"It is always the same wherever one is," complained the rose.

"To my eye, it is always changing," said the dove.

"I am weary of playing in this one spot forever," whimpered the fountain. "The same old patterns every day. Help, help, another spray!"

"There's nothing in the wood, I think, but horned owls in hollow oaks," the dove declared, "and violets by mossy stones."

"Violence by mossy stones is what I crave!" the fountain cried. "I'd love to meet the waterfall in silver combat, and damned be him who first dries up!"

"I have nothing to remember and nothing to forget," sighed the rose. "I waste my sweetness on the verdant air."

"I like it here" was all the dove would say. But the rose and the fountain kept after him every day of every week, and when the summer waned, they convinced the dove he loved the wood, admired horned owls, and ought to spend his life salvaging stars and meeting waterfalls in silver combat.

So the dove flew away into the wood and never came back. There were many varied rumors of the nature of his end. The four winds whispered that the dove had ceased to be because of mossy stones, half-hidden violets, or violence, malicious waterfalls, and owls in trees, but the wood thrush contended the dove had died while playing with burning stars. One thing was sure: the dove had ended the way no other dove had ever ended.

MORAL: *He who lives another's life another's death must die.*

The Bachelor Penguin
and the Virtuous Mate

ONE SPRING a bachelor penguin's fancy lightly turned, as it did in every season, to thoughts of illicit love. It was this gay seducer's custom to make passes at the more desirable females after their mates had gone down to the sea to fish. He had found out that all the females in the community made a ritual of rearranging the sitting-room furniture, putting it back where it had been the day before, and they were only too glad to have a strong male help them move the heavier pieces. Their mates had grown less and less interested in housework and more and more addicted to fishing, as time went on. The bachelor penguin proved handy at putting on or taking off screen doors, removing keys wedged in locks meant for other keys, and rescuing the females from other quandaries of their own making. After a few visits, the feathered Don Juan induced the ladies to play Hide-in-the-Dark with him, and Guess Who This Is?, and Webfooty-Webfooty.

As the seasons rolled on, the handsome and well-groomed Casanova became a little jaded by his routine successes with the opposite sex. Then one morning, after the other male penguins had gone to the seashore to fish as usual, Don J. Penguin spied the prettiest female he had ever seen, trying, all by herself, to move a sitting-room sofa back to the spot where it had been the day before. Don gallantly offered to help the matron in distress and she gladly accepted, with a shy look and a faint blush. The next morning the bachelor, who knew how to play his cards, came back and helped the housepenguin put on the screen door, and the following day he fixed the broken catch of her necklace, and the day after that he tightened the glass top of her percolator. Each time that he suggested playing Hide-in-the-Dark or Guess Who This Is?, the object of his desire thought of something else for him to fix, or loosen, or tighten, or take off, or put on. After several weeks of this, the amorist began to suspect that he was being taken, and his intended victim corroborated his fears.

"Unless you keep on helping me take things off, and put things on, and pry things loose, and make things tighter," she told the dismayed collector of broken hearts, "I will tell my mate about your improper advances and your dishonorable intentions." Don Penguin knew that the clever penguin's mate was the strongest male in the community, and also had the shortest temper and the least patience. There wasn't going to be any Hide-in-the-Dark or Guess Who This Is? or Webfooty-Webfooty. And so he spent the rest of his days working for the virtuous and guileful lady of his desire, moving sofas, taking things off and putting things on, loosening this and tightening that, and performing whatever other tasks his fair captor demanded of him. His bow tie became untied, his dinner jacket lost its buttons, his trousers lost their crease, and his eyes lost their dream. He babbled of clocks, and of keys caught in locks, and everybody closed her door when he came waddling down the street except the penguin who had taken him in with a beauty as unattainable as the stars, and a shy look, and a faint blush as phony as a parrot's laugh. One day her mate, returning early from the sea, caught a glimpse of Don leaving the house, and said, "What did old Droop Feather want?"

"Oh, he washes the windows and waxes the floors and sweeps the chimney," the female replied. "I believe he had an unhappy love affair."

MORAL: *One man's mate may sometimes be another man's prison.*

The Peacelike Mongoose

IN COBRA COUNTRY a mongoose was born one day who didn't want to fight cobras or anything else. The word spread from mongoose to mongoose that there was a mongoose who didn't want to fight cobras. If he didn't want to fight anything else, it was his own business, but it was the duty of every mongoose to kill cobras or be killed by cobras.

"Why?" asked the peacelike mongoose, and the word went around that the strange new mongoose was not only pro-cobra and anti-mongoose but intellectually curious and against the ideals and traditions of mongoosism.

"He is crazy," cried the young mongoose's father.

"He is sick," said his mother.

"He is a coward," shouted his brothers.

"He is a mongoosexual," whispered his sisters.

Strangers who had never laid eyes on the peacelike mongoose remembered that they had seen him crawling on his stomach, or trying on cobra hoods, or plotting the violent overthrow of Mongoosia.

"I am trying to use reason and intelligence," said the strange new mongoose.

"Reason is six-sevenths of treason," said one of his neighbors.

146

"Intelligence is what the enemy uses," said another.

Finally, the rumor spread that the mongoose had venom in his sting, like a cobra, and he was tried, convicted by a show of paws, and condemned to banishment.

MORAL: *Ashes to ashes, and clay to clay, if the enemy doesn't get you your own folks may.*

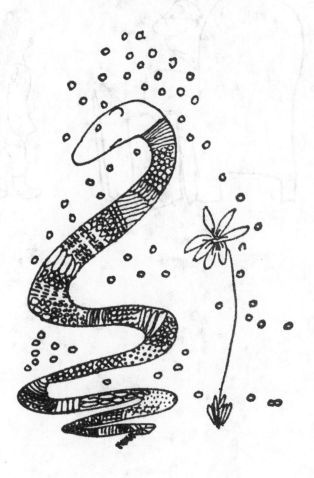

The Godfather
and His Godchild

A WORLDLY-WISE COLLECTOR, who had trotted the globe collecting everything he could shoot, or buy, or make off with, called upon his godchild, a little girl of five, after a year of collecting in various countries of the world.

"I want to give you three things," he said. "Any three things your heart desires. I have diamonds from Africa, and a rhinoceros horn, scarabs from Egypt, emeralds from Guatemala, chessmen of ivory and gold, mooses' antlers, signal drums, ceremonial gongs, temple bells, and three rare and remarkable dolls. Now tell me," he concluded, patting the little girl on the head, "what do you want more than anything else in the world?"

His little godchild, who was not a hesitater, did not hesitate. "I want to break your glasses and spit on your shoes," she said.

MORAL: *Though statisticians in our time have never kept score, Man wants a great deal here below and Woman even more.*

The Grizzly
and the Gadgets

A GRIZZLY BEAR who had been on a bender for several weeks following a Christmas party in his home at which his brother-in-law had set the Christmas tree on fire, his children had driven the family car through the front door and out the back, and all the attractive female bears had gone into hibernation before sunset returned home prepared to forgive, and live and let live. He found, to his mild annoyance, that the doorbell had been replaced by an ornamental knocker. When he lifted the knocker, he was startled to hear it play two bars of "Silent Night."

When nobody answered his knock, he turned the doorknob, which said "Happy New Year" in a metallic voice, and a two-tone gong rang "Hello" somewhere deep within the house.

He called to his mate, who was always the first to lay the old aside, as well as the first by whom the new was tried, and got no answer. This was because the walls of his house had been soundproofed by a soundproofer who had soundproofed them so well nobody could hear anybody say anything six feet away. Inside the living room the grizzly bear turned on the light switch, and the lights went on all right, but the

turning of the switch had also released an odor of pine cones, which this particular bear had always found offensive. The head of the house, now becoming almost as angry as he had been on Christmas Day, sank into an easy chair and began bouncing up and down and up and down, for it was a brand-new contraption called "Sitpretty" which made you bounce up and down and up and down when you sat on it. Now thoroughly exasperated, the bear jumped up from the chair and began searching for a cigarette. He found a cigarette box, a new-fangled cigarette box he had never seen before, which was made of metal and plastic in the shape of a castle, complete with portal and drawbridge and tower. The trouble was that the bear couldn't get the thing open. Then he made out, in tiny raised letters on the portal, a legend in rhyme: "You can have a cigarette on me if you can find the castle key." The bear could not find the castle key, and he threw the trick cigarette box through a windowpane out into the front yard, letting in a blast of cold air, and he howled when it hit the back of his neck. He was a little mollified when he found that he had a cigar in his pocket, but no matches, and so he began looking around the living room for a matchbox. At last he saw one on a shelf. There were matches in it, all right, but no scratching surface on which to scratch them. On the bottom of the box, however, there was a neat legend explaining this lack. The message on the box read: "Safety safety matches are doubly safe because there is no dangerous dangerous sandpaper surface to scratch them on. Strike them on a windowpane or on the seat of your pants."

Enraged, infuriated, beside himself, seeing red and thinking black, the grizzly bear began taking the living room apart. He pounded the matchbox into splinters, knocked over lamps, pulled pictures off the wall, threw rugs out of the broken window, swept vases and a clock off the mantelpiece, and overturned chairs and tables, growling and howling and roaring, shouting and bawling and cursing, until his wife was aroused from a deep dream of marrying a panda, neighbors appeared from blocks around, and the attractive female bears who had gone into hibernation began coming out of it to see what was going on.

The bear, deaf to the pleas of his mate, heedless of his neighbors' advice, and unafraid of the police, kicked over whatever was still standing in the house, and went roaring away for good, taking the most attractive of the attractive female bears, one named Honey, with him.

MORAL: *Nowadays most men lead lives of noisy desperation.*

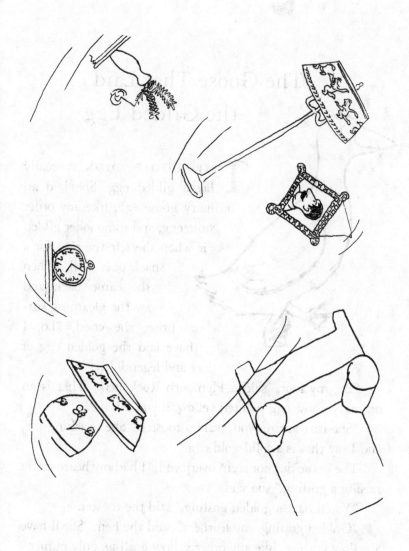

The Goose That Laid
the Gilded Egg

THE GOOSE DIDN'T really lay a gilded egg. She laid an ordinary goose egg, like any other goose egg, and some joker gilded it when she left the nest for a snack or a snail. When she came back and saw the gleaming surprise, she cried, "Lo, I have laid the golden egg of lore and legend!"

"Lo, my foot," said a Plymouth Rock hen. "That is an ordinary goose egg painted yellow, if you ask me."

"She isn't asking you," said a rooster. "She is asking me, and I say that is a solid-gold egg."

The goose did not seem overjoyed. "I had my heart set on raising a gosling," she said.

"You'll have a golden gosling," said the rooster.

"Golden gosling, my feathers," said the hen. "She'll have a yellow gosling, like any other yellow gosling, only punier."

154

"I don't care what it looks like," said the goose. "I just don't want it to be gold. People would talk. They would snatch my quills for souvenirs. I would be photographed all the time."

"I will offer you a fabulous sum for that glittering miracle," said the rooster, and he named a sum fabulous only as things are figured fiscally among the feathered. The goose gladly accepted the offer.

"I wouldn't sit on that egg," said the hen. "I wouldn't sit on it if a platinum gander encrusted with diamonds came out of it."

"I'll sit on it myself," said the rooster.

And so the hopeful rooster rolled the gilded goose egg to a nest and began sitting on it. At the end of three weeks, all the hens left his bed and board.

"You'll be sorry," said the rooster, "when this priceless treasure is hatched. I know it will be a golden goose. I have already named her—Goldie. When she becomes a full-grown goose, I will sell her to the highest bidder for a super-fabulous sum."

"Oh, sure," said the Plymouth Rock hen, "and my family came over on the Mayflower," and she went away.

The old positivist sat and sat and sat on the gilded egg, and all his friends drifted away, and no hen would look at him, and his feathers began to fall out. One day, being a male and not a female, he clumsily stepped on the egg and broke it, and that was the end of the egg and the end of his dreams.

MORAL: *It is wiser to be hendubious than cocksure.*

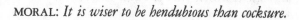

The Trial
of the Old Watchdog

A N OLD EXPERIENCED collie, who had been a faithful country watchdog for many years, was arrested one summer's day and accused of the first-degree murder of a lamb. Actually, the lamb had been slain by a notorious red fox who had planted the still-warm body of his victim in the collie's kennel.

The trial was held in a kangaroo court presided over by Judge Wallaby. The jury consisted of foxes, and all the spectators were foxes. A fox named Reynard was prosecuting attorney. "Morning, Judge," he said.

"God bless you, boy, and good luck," replied Judge Wallaby jovially.

A poodle named Beau, an old friend and neighbor of the collie, represented the accused watchdog. "Good morning, Judge," said the poodle.

"Now I don't want you to be too clever," the Judge warned him. "Cleverness should be confined to the weaker side. That's only fair."

A blind woodchuck was the first creature to take the stand, and she testified that she saw the collie kill the lamb.

"The witness is blind!" protested the poodle.

"No personalities, please," said the Judge severely. "Perhaps the witness saw the murder in a dream or a vision. This would give her testimony the authority of revelation."

"I wish to call a character witness," said the poodle.

"We have no character witnesses," said Reynard smoothly, "but we have some charming character assassins."

One of these, a fox named Burrows, was called to the stand. "I didn't actually see this lamb killer kill this lamb," said Burrows, "but I almost did."

"That's close enough," said Judge Wallaby.

"Objection," barked the poodle.

"Objection overruled," said the Judge. "It's getting late. Has the jury reached a verdict?"

The forefox of the jury stood up. "We find the defendant guilty," he said, "but we think it would be better to acquit him, nonetheless. If we hang the defendant, his punishment will be over. But if we acquit him of such dark crimes as murder, concealing the body, and associating with poodles and defense attorneys, nobody will ever trust him again, and he will be suspect all the days of his life. Hanging is too good for him, and much too quick."

"Guilt by exoneration!" Reynard cried. "What a lovely way to end his usefulness!"

And so the case was dismissed and court was adjourned, and everybody went home to tell about it.

MORAL: *Thou shalt not blindfold justice by pulling the wool over her eyes.*

The Philosopher
and the Oyster

B Y THE SEA on a lovely morning strolled a
philosopher—one who seeks a magnificent explanation
for his insignificance—and there he came upon an oyster lying in its shell upon the sand.

"It has no mind to be burdened by doubt," mused the
philosopher, "no fingers to work to the bone. It can never say,
'My feet are killing me.' It hears no evil, sees no television,
speaks no folly. It has no buttons to come off, no zipper to get
caught, no hair or teeth to fall out." The philosopher sighed a
deep sigh of envy. "It produces a highly lustrous concretion, of

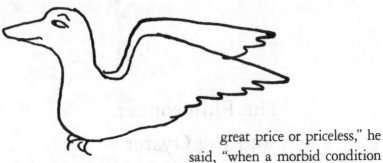

great price or priceless," he said, "when a morbid condition obtains in its anatomy, if you could call such an antic, anomalous amorphousness anatomy." The philosopher sighed again and said, "Would that I could wake from delirium with a circlet of diamonds upon my fevered brow. Would, moreover, that my house were my sanctuary, as sound and secure as a safe-deposit vault."

Just then a screaming sea gull swooped out of the sky, picked up the oyster in its claws, carried it high in the air, and let it drop upon a great wet rock, shattering the shell and splattering its occupant. There was no lustrous concretion, of any price whatever, among the debris, for the late oyster had been a very healthy oyster, and, anyway, no oyster ever profited from its pearl.

MORAL: *Count your own blessings, and let your neighbor count his. Where there is no television, the people also perish.*

Tea for One

A YOUNG HUSBAND was wakened at five o'clock one morning by his bride. "Is the house on fire?" he mumbled. She laughed merrily. "The dawn is here," she said, "and I am going to bake a sugar cake."

"I don't want a sugar cake, I want toast and coffee," the bridegroom said.

"The sugar cake's for you to take for all the boys to see," she explained.

"All what boys?" demanded her husband, who was still drowsy.

"The boys at the office, silly," she said. "Let them see it, and then bring it home, and maybe we'll have it for dinner."

He got up and started to dress.

"I'll make tea for both of us now," she said, singing the line, and adding, "Coffee doesn't rhyme with anything. You can't have coffee."

He had tied his shoes and was tying his tie, when her voice brightened and she clapped her hands. "We'll raise a family," she said gaily. "You can have the boy, and I'll take the girl." And she scampered down the stairs to start to bake the sugar cake for him to take for all the boys to see. When she had gone, the bridegroom glanced at his watch. It was eleven minutes after five. He brushed his teeth and combed his hair, and then he climbed out the bedroom window, dropped to the ground below, and slipped away into the dawn, to find an all-night restaurant where a man could get a meal a man could eat.

MORAL: *If life went along like a popular song, every man's marriage would surely go wrong.*

The Mouse
and the Money

A CITY MOUSE who moved to the country to live in the walls of an old house with a lot of country mice began lording it over them from the start. He trimmed his whiskers, put *mousseline* in his hair, talked with an accent, and told the country mice that they came from the wrong side of the mouse tracks.

"My ancestors were of the French aristocracy," boasted the city mouse. "Our name still appears on bottles of great French wine: *Mise du château*, which means mice in the chateau, or castle mice." Every day the newcomer bragged about his forebears, and when he ran out of ancestors he made some up. "My great-great-great-grandfather was a theater mouse at the Comédie-Française, and he married a cathedral mouse, one of the cathedral mice of Chartres. At their wedding a dessert named in their honor, *mousse chocolat*, was served to millions of guests."

Then the city mouse told how his family had come to America in the bridal suite of a great French liner. "My brother is a restaurant mouse at '21,' and my sister's at the Metropolitan," he said. He went on to tell of other ancestors of the family who had been in such productions as *The Chauve Souris* and *Die Fledermaus* and *Les Trois Mousquetaires*. "Not a mouse in our house was a common house mouse," he said.

One day, wandering through forbidden walls of the country house, to show his inferiors that he knew his way around, he came upon a treasure in currency which someone had hidden years before between the plaster and the lath. "I wouldn't eat that stuff," warned an old country mouse. "It is the root of evil and it will give you greenback bellyache." But the city mouse did not listen.

"I'm already a mouse of distinction," said the city mouse, "and this money will make me a millionaire. I'll be loaded." So he began to eat the currency, which consisted of bills of large denominations, and he drove off one or two of the young country mice who wanted to help him eat the treasure, saying, "Finders are not their brothers' keepers." The city mouse told his country cousins, "Blessed are

the rich, for they can pay their way into the kingdom of Heaven," and he got off a lot of other witticisms, such as "Legal tender is the night" and "Money makes the nightmare go."

And so he went on living, as he put it, on the fat of the lath. "When I have eaten it all," he said, "I shall return to the city and live like a king. They say you can't take it with you, but I'm going to take it with *me*."

In a few days and nights the arrogant city mouse with the fancy and fanciful French forebears had eaten all the money, which amounted to an ambassador's annual salary. Then he tried to leave the walls of the old country house, but he was so loaded with money, and his head was so swelled, that he got caught between the plaster and the lath and could not get out, his neighbors could not dislodge him, and so he died in the walls, and nobody but the country mice knew that he had been the richest mouse in the world.

MORAL: *This is the posture of fortune's slave: one foot in the gravy, one foot in the grave.*

The Wolf
at the Door

MR. AND MRS. SHEEP were sitting in their sitting room with their daughter, who was as pretty as she was edible, when there was a knock at the front door. "It's a gentleman caller," said the daughter.

"It's the Fuller Brush man," said her mother. The cautious father got up and looked out the window. "It's the wolf," he said. "I can see his tail."

"Don't be silly," said the mother. "It's the Fuller Brush man, and that's his brush." And she went to the door and opened it, and the wolf came in and ran away with the daughter.

"You were right, after all," admitted the mother, sheepishly.

MORAL: *Mother doesn't* always *know best. (The italics are father's and daughter's and mine.)*

What Happened
to Charles

A FARM HORSE named Charles was led to town one
day by his owner, to be shod. He would have been shod
and brought back home without incident if it hadn't been
for Eva, a duck, who was always hanging about the kitchen
door of the farmhouse, eavesdropping, and never got anything quite right. Her farmmates said of her that she had two
mouths but only one ear.

On the day that Charles was led away to the smithy, Eva
went quacking about the farm, excitedly telling the other
animals that Charles had been taken to town to be shot.

"They're executing an innocent horse!" cried Eva. "He's a
hero! He's a martyr! He died to make us free!"

"He was the greatest horse in the world," sobbed a sentimental hen.

"He just seemed like old Charley to me," said a realistic
cow. "Let's not get into a moony mood."

"He was wonderful!" cried a gullible goose.

"What did he ever do?" asked a goat.

Eva, who was as inventive as she was inaccurate, turned
on her lively imagination. "It was butchers who led him off

168

to be shot!" she shrieked. "They would have cut our throats while we slept if it hadn't been for Charles!"

"I didn't see any butchers, and I can see a burnt-out fire-fly on a moonless night," said a barn owl. "I didn't hear any butchers, and I can hear a mouse walk across moss."

"We must build a memorial to Charles the Great, who saved our lives," quacked Eva. And all the birds and beasts in the barnyard except the wise owl, the skeptical goat, and the realistic cow set about building a memorial.

Just then the farmer appeared in the lane, leading Charles, whose new shoes glinted in the sunlight.

It was lucky that Charles was not alone, for the memorial-builders might have set upon him with clubs and stones for replacing their hero with just plain old Charley. It was lucky, too, that they could not reach the barn owl, who quickly perched upon the weathervane of the barn, for none is so exasperating as he who is right. The sentimental hen and the gullible goose were the ones who finally called attention to the true culprit—Eva, the one-eared duck with two mouths.

The others set upon her and tarred and unfeathered her, for none is more unpopular than the bearer of sad tidings that turn out to be false.

MORAL: *Get it right or let it alone. The conclusion you jump to may be your own.*

The Daws
on the Dial

A YOUNG JACKDAW* told his father that he was going to build his nest on the minute hand of the town
clock. "That's the most unthinkable thing you ever thought
of," said old John Daw. Young Jack was not deterred. "We'll
build our nest when the minute hand is level," he said, "at a
quarter of or a quarter after."

"Those who live in castles in the air have nowhere to
go but down," the old Daw warned, but Jack and his mate
built their nest on the clock at a quarter after eight the next
morning. At twenty minutes after eight the nest slipped off
the minute hand and fell into the street below. "We didn't
start early enough," the young Daw told his father that evening. "Better never than late. We'll try again tomorrow at a
quarter after six."

"If at first you don't succeed, fail, fail again," said the
elder Daw. But he might as well have been talking to a
gargoyle. Jack and his mate stole some of the elder Daw's
silverware and built their nest again the following morning,

---

* A species of crow associated with the idea of thieving.

and again it slipped off the minute hand and fell into the street below.

That evening old John Daw had more to say to his reckless offspring. "To stick on a dial, you would need three feet, one of them a rabbit's. Don't hang heavy on time's hands, just because it hangs heavy on yours. Clockwise is not wise enough. Even the cyclone and the merry-go-round know that much."

And again the young Daws did not listen, and again they swiped some silverware from his parents' nest to furnish their own. This time, those human beings known as municipal authorities were concealed in the clock tower, and, with brooms and yells and stones and bells, they frightened the foolish Daws away from the clock and the tower and the town.

That night old John Daw's mate counted her silverware and sighed with dismay. "Gone, alas, with our youth, two spoons," she said, "and half the knives, and most of the forks, and all of the napkin rings."

"If I told him once, I told him a hundred times, 'Neither a burglar nor a lender be,'" raged old John, "but I might as well have been talking to a cast-iron lawn Daw." Not a word was heard from the young Daws as the weeks went on. "No news is bad news," grumbled old John Daw. "They have probably built their nest this time on a wagon wheel, or inside a bell."

He was wrong about that. The young Daws had built their last nest in the muzzle of a cannon, and they heard only the first gun of a twenty-one-gun salute fired in honor of a visiting chief of state.

MORAL: *The saddest words of pen or tongue*
are wisdom's wasted on the young.

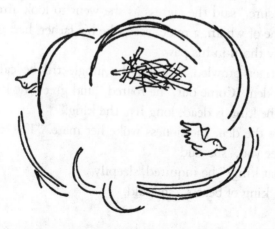

The Tiger
Who Would Be King

ONE MORNING THE tiger woke up in the jungle and told his mate that he was king of beasts.

"Leo, the lion, is king of beasts," she said.

"We need a change," said the tiger. "The creatures are crying for a change."

The tigress listened but she could hear no crying, except that of her cubs.

"I'll be king of beasts by the time the moon rises," said the tiger. "It will be a yellow moon with black stripes, in my honor."

"Oh, sure," said the tigress as she went to look after her young, one of whom, a male, very like his father, had got an imaginary thorn in his paw.

The tiger prowled through the jungle till he came to the lion's den. "Come out," he roared, "and greet the king of beasts! The king is dead, long live the king!"

Inside the den, the lioness woke her mate. "The king is here to see you," she said.

"What king?" he inquired, sleepily.

"The king of beasts," she said.

"I am the king of beasts," roared Leo, and he charged out of the den to defend his crown against the pretender.

It was a terrible fight, and it lasted until the setting of the sun. All the animals of the jungle joined in, some taking the side of the tiger and others the side of the lion. Every creature from the aardvark to the zebra took part in the struggle to overthrow the lion or to repulse the tiger, and some did not know which they were fighting for, and some fought for both, and some fought whoever was nearest, and some fought for the sake of fighting.

"What are we fighting for?" someone asked the aardvark.

"The old order," said the aardvark.

"What are we dying for?" someone asked the zebra.

"The new order," said the zebra.

When the moon rose, fevered and gibbous, it shone upon a jungle in which nothing stirred except a macaw and a cockatoo, screaming in horror. All the beasts were dead except the tiger, and his days were numbered and his time was ticking away. He was monarch of all he surveyed, but it didn't seem to mean anything.

MORAL: *You can't very well be king of beasts if there aren't any.*

The Chipmunk
and His Mate

A MALE CHIPMUNK could sleep like a top or a log or a baby as soon as his head hit the pillow, but his mate was always as wakeful as an owl or a nightwatchman or a burglar. When he turned the lights off, she would turn them on again and read, or worry, or write letters in her head, or wonder where things were. She was often drowsy after supper, and sometimes nodded in her chair, but she became wide awake as soon as her head hit the pillow. She would lie there wondering if her mate had left his pistol in the nursery, what she had done with the Christmas tree ornaments, and whether or not she had left the fire on under the prunes. She was sure the wastebasket was smoldering in the living room, that she had left the kitchen door unlocked, and that someone was tiptoeing around downstairs.

The male chipmunk always slept until the sun was high, but his mate heard all the clocks strike all the hours. She could doze off in the daytime with a glass in her hand, or while her mate was reading aloud, or when his boss came to call, but as soon as she got in bed, she began writing letters in her head, or wondering if she had put the cat out, or where her handbag was, or why she hadn't heard from her mother.

One day she fell asleep while driving the family car, and, after a decent interval, the male chipmunk married her sister. He could still sleep like a top or a log or a baby, but his new mate just lay there as wide awake as an owl or a night-watchman or a burglar, hearing intruders, smelling something burning, wondering if her mate had let his insurance lapse. One enchanted evening, across a crowded room, he met a stranger, an eight o'clock sleepy-time gal. They ran away to Maracaibo together, where they slept happily ever after. The second mate lay awake every night, wondering what the chipfrump had that she didn't have and what he saw in her, and whether she herself had put out the milk bottles or left the water running in the kitchen sink.

MORAL: *A man's bed is his cradle,*
but a woman's is often her rack.

The Weaver
and the Worm

A WEAVER WATCHED in wide-eyed wonder a silk-worm spinning its cocoon in a white mulberry tree.

"Where do you get that stuff?" asked the admiring weaver.

"Do you want to make something out of it?" inquired the silkworm, eagerly.

Then the weaver and the silkworm went their separate ways, for each thought the other had insulted him. We live, man and worm, in a time when almost everything can mean almost anything, for this is the age of gobbledygook, double-talk, and gudda.

MORAL: *A word to the wise is not sufficient if it doesn't make any sense.*

179

Two Dogs

ONE SULTRY MOONLESS night, a leopard escaped from a circus and slunk away into the shadows of a city. The chief of police dogs assigned to the case a German shepherd named Plunger and a plainclothes bloodhound named Plod. Plod was a slow, methodical sleuth, but his uniformed partner was restless and impatient. Plod set the pace until Plunger snapped, "We couldn't catch a turtle this way," and bounded along the trail like a whippet. He got lost. When Plod found him, half an hour later, the bloodhound said, "It is better to get somewhere slowly than nowhere fast."

"Repose is for the buried," said the police dog. "I even chase cats in my dreams."

"I don't," said the bloodhound. "Out of scent, out of mind."

As they went along, each in his own way, through the moonlessness, they exchanged further observations on life.

"He who hunts and turns away may live to hunt another day," commented Plod.

"*Runs* away, you mean," sneered Plunger.

"I never run," said the bloodhound. "It's no good trailing a cat when you're out of breath, especially if the cat isn't. I figured that out myself. They call it instinct."

"I was taught to do what I do, and not to do what I don't," the police dog said. "They call it discipline. When *I* catch cats, cats stay caught," he added.

"I don't catch them, I merely find out where they are," the bloodhound said quietly.

The two dogs suddenly made out a great dark house looming in front of them at the end of a lane. "The trail ends right here, twenty feet from that window," the bloodhound said, sniffing a certain spot. "The leopard must have leaped into the house from here."

The two dogs stared into the open window of the dark and silent house.

"I was taught to jump through the open windows of dark houses," said Plunger.

"I taught myself not to," said Plod. "I wouldn't grab that cat if I were you. I never grab a leopard unless it is a coat." But Plunger wasn't listening.

"Here goes," he said jauntily, and he jumped through the window of the dark and silent house. Instantly there was a racket that sounded to the keen ears of the bloodhound like a police dog being forcibly dressed in women's clothes by a leopard, and that is precisely what it was. All of a moment, Plunger, dressed in women's clothes from hat to shoes, with a pink parasol thrust under his collar, came hurtling out the window. "I had my knee on his chest, too," said the bewildered police dog plaintively.

The old sleuth sighed. "He lasteth longest and liveth best who gets not his knee on his quarry's chest," murmured Plod, in cloudy English but fluent Bloodhound.

MORAL: *Who would avoid life's wriest laughter should not attain the thing he's after.*

The Lady of the Legs

IN A POOL near Paris there lived a frog who thought she was wonderful.

"I have the largest lily pad, the deepest dive, the prettiest eyes, and the finest voice in the world," she croaked.

"You also have the most succulent legs on earth or water," said a human voice one day. It was the voice of a renowned Parisian restaurateur, who was passing by when he heard all the bragging.

"I do not know what succulent means," said the frog.

"You must have the smallest vocabulary in the world," said the restaurateur, and the foolish frog, who took every superlative for praise, was pleased, and flushed a deeper green than ever.

"I should like to set you before a certain celebrated *bon vivant*," said the man, "a distinguished gourmet, a connoisseur of the *grande haute cuisine*."

The frog almost swooned with delight at the elegant sound of these strange words.

"You will be served like a queen," said the restaurateur. "Provençal. Under my personal supervision, of course."

"Tell me more," said the rapt and rapturous frog.

"You will be served with the most excellent vintage wine in the world," said the man. "A great Montrachet, I should think, would be perfect."

"Go on," urged the vain and foolish frog.

"You will be talked about whenever devotees of the culinary art assemble," said the restaurateur. "You will be remembered as the daintiest dish in the history of gastronomy."

At this the frog swooned in a transport of joy and an excess of misplaced self-esteem, and while she was unconscious, the renowned Parisian restaurateur deftly removed her succulent legs and took them to his restaurant, where they were prepared under his personal supervision as he had promised, and served, Provençal, with a bottle of Montrachet, to a celebrated *bon vivant*.

MORAL: *Fatua cruraque mox separabuntur.**

---

*   Playing off the proverb "A fool and his money will soon be parted," Thurber's Latin can be translated as "A fool(ish lady) and her legs will soon be parted."

The Kingfisher
and the Phoebe

A PROUD MOTHER phoebe who had raised two broods of fledglings in the fair weather was at first dismayed and then delighted when one of the males of the second brood refused to leave the nest and fly away like the others. "I have raised a remarkable phoebe unlike any other phoebe," the mother bird decided. "He will become a great singer, greater than the nightingale."

She brought in a nightingale to teach her son to sing, and then a catbird, and then a mockingbird, but all the young phoebe could learn to sing was "Phoebe, Phoebe." And so the mother bird sent for Dr. Kingfisher, a bird psychologist, who examined the young phoebe carefully.

"This phoebe is a phoebe like any other phoebe," he told the mother. "And all he will ever sing is 'Phoebe, Phoebe.'"

But the ambitious mother did not believe Dr. Kingfisher's prognosis. "Maybe he won't be a great singer, but he will be a great something," she insisted. "He will take the place of the eagle on the dollar, or the canary in the gilded cage, or the cuckoo in the cuckoo clock. You just wait."

"I'll wait," said Dr. Kingfisher, and he waited. But nothing happened. The phoebe went on being a phoebe and singing "Phoebe, Phoebe" like any other phoebe, and that was all.

MORAL: *You can't make anything out of cookie dough except cookies.*

The Turtle
Who Conquered Time

A TURTLE APPEARED in a meadow one summer's day and attracted the attention of all the creatures in the grass and in the trees, because the date 44 B.C. was carved on his shell. "Our meadow is honored indeed," exclaimed a grasshopper, "for our visitor is the oldest of all living creatures."

"We must build a pavilion in his honor," said a frog, and the catbirds and the swallows and the other birds built a stately pleasure dome out of twigs and leaves and blossoms for the very important turtle. An orchestra of crickets played music in his honor, and a wood thrush sang. The sounds of jubilee were heard in nearby fields and woods, and as more and more creatures turned up from farther and farther away to have a look at the ancient turtle, the grasshopper decided to charge admission to the pavilion.

"I will be the barker," said the frog, and, with the help of the grasshopper, he composed an impressive spiel. "Yesterday and yesterday and yesterday," it began, "creeps in this carapace from day to day to the first syllable of recorded time. This great turtle was born two thousand years ago, the year the mighty Julius Caesar died. Horace was twenty-one in 44

B.C., and Cicero had but a single year to live." The bystanders did not seem very much interested in the turtle's ancient contemporaries, but they gladly paid to go in and have a look at his ancient body.

Inside the pavilion, the grasshopper continued the lecture. "This remarkable turtle is a direct descendant of one of the first families of Ooze," he chanted. "His great-grandfather may have been the first thing that moved in the moist and muddy margins of this cooling planet. Except for our friend's ancestors, there was nothing but coal and blobs of glob."

One day a red squirrel who lived in a neighboring wood dropped in to look at the turtle and to listen to the ballyhoo. "Forty-four B.C., my foot!" scoffed the squirrel, as he glared at the grasshopper. "You are full of tobacco juice, and your friend the frog is full of lightning bugs. The carving of an ancient date on the carapace of a turtle is a common childish prank. This creep was probably born no earlier than 1902."

As the red squirrel ranted on, the spectators who had paid to get into the pavilion began departing quietly, and there was no longer a crowd listening to the frog out front. The crickets put away their instruments and disappeared as silently as the Arabs, and the wood thrush gathered up his sheet music and flew off and did not return. The sounds of jubilee were no longer heard in the once merry meadow, and the summer seemed to languish like a dying swan.

"I knew all the time he wasn't two thousand years old," admitted the grasshopper, "but the legend pleased the people, young and old, and many smiled who had not smiled for years."

"And many laughed who had not laughed for years," said the frog, "and many eyes sparkled and many hearts were gay." The turtle shed a turtle tear at this and crawled away.

"The truth is not merry and bright," said the red squirrel. "The truth is cold and dark. Let's face it." And, looking smug and superior, the iconoclast scampered impudently back to his tree in the wood. From the grass of the meadow voices once carefree and gay joined in a rueful and lonely chorus, as if someone great and wonderful had died and was being buried.

MORAL: *Oh, why should the shattermyth have to be a crumplehope and a dampenglee?*

The Lion
and the Lizard

A LION AND a lizard kept the halls where once a prince
had slept. The prince had died, as even princes do, and
his palace had fallen to rats and ruin. The lion destroyed the
rats, but he could never find the lizard, who lived in a crevice in the wall. There was royal food in the ruined kitchen,
and royal wine in the ruined cellar, but the lion got it all,
for the lizard was afraid to emerge from his hiding place. So
the lion got fatter and fatter, and drunker and drunker, and
the lizard grew thinner and thinner, and soberer and soberer.
Weeks went by, and the weeds grew and the walls crumbled,
as the lion ate six meals a day, washing them down with a
total of eighteen different wines. One night, as the tawny
master of the palace was topping off his sixth meal of the
day with a tankard of brandy, he fell asleep on his golden
chair at the head of the ornate table. The lizard, with his
remaining strength, which wasn't much, crawled up on the
table and tried to nibble a crumb, but he was too weak to eat.
The lion, awakened by a tiny tinkle of spoons, tried to crush
the unwelcome guest with one blow of his mighty paw, but

he was sated and obese, and his paw was no longer mighty. He passed away in his golden chair, spilling the last of the brandy, as the lizard gave up the ghost among the crumbs and silver.

MORAL: *He who dies of a surfeit is as dead as he who starves.*

The Tigress
and Her Mate

PROUDFOOT, A TIGER, became tired of his mate, Sabra, a few weeks after they had set up housekeeping, and he fell to leaving home earlier and earlier in the morning, and returning later and later at night. He no longer called her "Sugar Paw," or anything else, but merely clapped his paws when he wanted anything, or, if she was upstairs, whistled. The last long speech he ever made to her at breakfast was "What the hell's the matter with you? I bring you rice and peas and coconut oil, don't I? Love is something you put away in the attic with your wedding dress. Forget it." And he finished his coffee, put down the *Jungle News*, and started for the door.

"Where are you going?" Sabra asked.

"Out," he said. And after that, every time she asked him where he was going, he said, "Out," or "Away," or "Hush."

When Sabra became aware of the coming of what would have been, had she belonged to the chosen species, a blessed event, and told Proudfoot about it, he snarled, "Growp." He had now learned to talk to his mate in code, and "growp"

meant "I hope the cubs grow up to be xylophone players or major generals." Then he went away, as all male tigers do at such a moment, for he did not want to be bothered by his young until the males were old enough to box with and the females old enough to insult. While waiting for the unblessed event to take place, he spent his time fighting water buffaloes and riding around with plainclothes tigers in a prowl car.

When he finally came home, he said to his mate, "Eeps," meaning "I'm going to hit the sack, and if the kids keep me awake by yowling, I'll drown them like so many common house kittens." Sabra stalked to the front door of their house, opened it, and said to her mate, "Scat." The fight that took place was terrible but brief. Proudfoot led with the wrong paw, was nailed with the swiftest right cross in the jungle, and never really knew where he was after that. The next morning, when the cubs, male and female, tumbled eagerly down the stairs demanding to know what they could do, their mother said, "You can go in the parlor and play with your father. He's the tiger rug just in front of the fireplace. I hope you'll like him."

The children loved him.

MORAL: *Never be mean to a tiger's wife, especially if you're the tiger.*

The Magpie's
Treasure

ONE DAY WHEN the sun made everything that glitters glitter and everything that sparkles sparkle, a magpie picked up something from a gutter and carried it off to her nest. A crow and a rabbit had seen her swoop down and fly away, and each decided she had found something good to eat. "I'm sure it's a carrot," said the rabbit, "for I heard her say something about carrots."

"I saw it glitter," said the crow, "and it glittered edibly, like a yellow grain of corn."

"Corn is for the commoner," said the rabbit scornfully.

"You can have your carrots, and welcome to them," said the crow. They smacked their lips as they approached the magpie's nest. "I'll find out what she's got," said the crow. "If it's a grain of corn, I'll eat it. If it's a carrot, I'll throw it down to you."

So the crow flew to the edge of the magpie's nest while the rabbit waited below. The magpie happily showed the crow what she had found in the gutter. "It's a fourteen-carat diamond set in a golden ring," she said. "I wanted rings from the time I could fly, but my parents were worm collectors. If

I had had my way, I'd be a wealthy bird today, surrounded by rings and other lovely things."

"You are living in the pluperfect subjunctive," said the crow disdainfully.

"It's serene there, and never crowded, except for old regrets," the magpie said.

The crow dropped down to the ground and explained to the rabbit that the "carrots" the magpie had talked about were only carats. "One carrot is worth fourteen carats," the rabbit said. "You can multiply that by twenty and it will still be true."

"If I can't eat it, I don't want it," said the crow. "Seeing is deceiving. It's eating that's believing." And the crow and the rabbit swallowed their disappointment, for want of anything else, and left the magpie to the enjoyment of her treasure.

The light made everything that sparkles sparkle, and everything that glitters glitter, and the magpie was content until the setting of the sun.

> MORAL: Chacun à son gout* *is very very true, but why should we despise the apples of other eyes?*

---

*   The French translates as "to each his own taste."

The Cricket
and the Wren

AT A MUSIC festival one summer in Tangletale Wood, a score of soloists came together to compete for the annual Peacock Awards. The Cricket was asked to pick the winner because of his fame as a fiddler and his many appearances on radio, where he is employed to let audiences know when it is night.

The Cricket was met at the station by the Wren, who flew him to an inn, bought him a drink, carried his bags upstairs to his room, and was in general so courteous and attentive that the Cricket thought he was the proprietor of the inn.

"I am not a proprietor, but a competitor," the Wren said. "It is a greater honor to be judged by you, even if I should lose, than to win the highest award from a lesser critic and cricket. As small tokens of my esteem, here are a bottle of wine and a cherry pie, and the key to the boudoir of as charming a lady cricket as you would attract in a year of chirping."

That afternoon, the Wren flew the Cricket out to the

concert field, where he heard the Frog scrape his cello, the Lark blow his clarion trumpet, the Nightingale strum his lyre of gold, the Blackbird play his boxwood flute, the Catbird run his bright piano arpeggios, and the Partridge show off on his drums. The vocalists came next, beginning with the Canary, a temperamental visitor from abroad, who had sat up all night bragging of his ability and was, as a consequence, in lousy voice. "The Owl can do better than that even if all he can sing is 'Who,'" said the Wren, who had slipped quietly into a chair next to the Cricket's. He gave the critic a cigar, a light, and a swig from a flask. "I shall sing a group of *Lieder*," said the Wren, "all of them Henley's 'Take, Dear, This Little Sheaf of Songs.' I composed the music myself, and dedicated it to my mate and to you."

The Mockingbird sang next, and those in the audience who hoped the amiable Wren would win with his bright little group of songs, all of them the same song, began to worry, for the Mockingbird had slept all night, dreaming of victory, and as a consequence, was in heavenly voice. "I should say his tongue is sharp rather than sweet," whispered the Wren. "When I told him last night that you were a finer fiddler than all the finest fiddlers in the field, he remarked that, to him, you looked like a limousine come to grief at an intersection."

The Cricket rubbed his legs together angrily, producing two low, ominous notes. "In my opinion," the Wren went on, "you look like a shining piece of mechanism, handsome and authoritative, such as the trigger action of a Colt. Here is a lozenge for your cough, and a pillow for your chair, and a footstool for your feet."

When it came time for the Wren to sing, his group of songs, all of them the same song, delighted everybody in the audience except the other soloists and their friends and families.

"I could do better than that," sneered the Mockingbird, "with my beak closed."

"I have thrashed singers with voices ten times better than that," said the Brown Thrasher.

"*Gott im Himmel!*" cried the Canary. "*Er klingt wie ein rostiges eisernes Tor das geölt werden muss.*"*

In awarding first prize to the Wren, the Cricket said, in part and in parting, "His voice is like some bright piece of mechanism, such as the works of a golden music box, and he gives his group of one song an infinite variety. This artist also has a keen appreciation of values and a fine critical perception."

In departing, or, to be precise, escaping from, the music festival, the Cricket was fortunate enough to have at his disposal a private airplane, none other than the victorious Wren himself.

> MORAL: *It is not always more blessed to give than to receive, but it is frequently more rewarding.*

---

* The German translates as, "God in heaven! It sounds like a rusty iron gate that needs to be oiled."

The Crow
and the Scarecrow

ONCE UPON A farm an armada of crows descended like the wolf on the fold. They were after the seeds in the garden and the corn in the field. The crows posted sentinels, who warned them of the approach of the farmer, and they even had an undercover crow or two who mingled with the chickens in the barnyard and the pigeons on the roof, and found out the farmer's plans in advance. Thus they were able to raid the garden and the field when he was away, and they stayed hidden when he was at home. The farmer decided to build a scarecrow so terrifying it would scare the hateful crows to death when they got a good look at it. But the scarecrow, for all the work the farmer put in on it, didn't frighten even the youngest and most fluttery female. The marauders knew that the scarecrow was a suit of old clothes stuffed with straw and that what it held in its wooden hand was not a rifle but only a curtain rod.

As more and more corn and more and more seeds disappeared, the farmer became more and more eager for vengeance. One night, he made himself up to look like a scarecrow and in the dark, for it was a moonless night, his son helped him to take the place of the scarecrow. This time, however, the hand that held the gun was not made of wood and the gun was not an unloaded curtain rod, but a double-barrelled 12-gauge Winchester.

Dawn broke that morning with a sound like a thousand tin pans falling. This was the rebel yell of the crows coming down on field and garden like Jeb Stuart's* cavalry. Now one of the young crows who had been out all night, drinking corn instead of eating it, suddenly went into a tailspin, plunged into a bucket of red paint that was standing near the barn, and burst into flames.

The farmer was just about to blaze away at the squadron of crows with both barrels when the one that was on fire headed straight for him. The sight of a red crow, dripping what seemed to be blood, and flaring like a Halloween torch, gave the living scarecrow such a shock that he dropped dead in one beat less than the tick of a watch (which is the way we all want to go, *mutatis*, it need scarcely be said, *mutandis*).†

The next Sunday the parson preached a disconsolate sermon, denouncing drink, carryings on, adult delinquency,

---

* A Confederate general known for his cavalry raids.
† A Latin idiom meaning "when necessary changes have been made."

front-page marriages, golf on Sunday, adultery, careless handling of firearms, and cruelty to our feathered friends. After the sermon, the dead farmer's wife explained to the preacher what had really happened, but he only shook his head and murmured skeptically, "Confused indeed would be the time in which the crow scares the scarecrow and becomes the scarescarecrow."

MORAL: *All men kill the thing they hate, too,*
unless, of course, it kills them first.

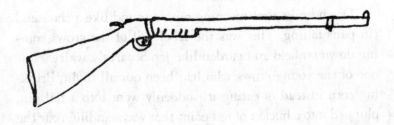

Ivory, Apes,
and People

A BAND OF ambitious apes in Africa once called upon
a herd of elephants with a business proposition. "We
can sell your tusks to people for a fortune in peanuts and
oranges," said the leader of the apes. "Tusks are tusks to
you and us, but to people they are merchandise—billiard
balls and piano keys and other things that people buy and
sell." The elephants said they would think it over. "Be
here tomorrow at this time and we will swing the deal,"
said the leader of the apes, and the apes went away to call
on some people who were hunting for merchandise in the
region.

"It's the very best ivory," the leader of the apes told the
leader of the people. "One hundred elephants, two hundred
tusks. All yours for oranges and peanuts."

"That's enough ivory for a small ivory tower," said the
leader of the people, "or four hundred billiard balls and a
thousand piano keys. I will cable my agent to ship your nuts
and oranges, and to sell the billiard balls and piano keys. The
business of business is business, and the heart of the matter
is speed."

"We will close the deal," said the leader of
the apes.

"Where is the merchandise now?" inquired the leader of the people.

"It's eating, or mating, but it will be
at the appointed place at the appointed
hour," replied the chief ape. But it
wasn't. The elephants had thought it
over, and reconsidered, and they forgot to show up the following day,
for elephants are good at forgetting
when forgetting is good. There was
a great to-do in the marts of world
trade when the deal fell through, and
everybody, except the elephants, got
into the litigation that followed: the
Better Business Bureau, the Monkey Business Bureau, the Interspecies
Commerce Commission, the federal
courts, the National Association of
Merchandisers, the African Bureau of
Investigation, the International Association for the Advancement of Animals,
and the American Legion. Opinions
were handed down, rules were promul-
gated, subpoenas were issued, injunctions
were granted and denied, and objections were
sustained and overruled. The Patriotic League of American
Women Against Subversion took an active part until it was
denounced as subversive by a man who later withdrew his

accusation and made a fortune on the sale of two books, *I Made My Bed* and *I Lie in My Teeth*.

The elephants kept their ivory, and nobody got any billiard balls or piano keys, or a single nut or an orange.

MORAL: *Men of all degrees should form this prudent habit:*
never serve a rabbit stew before you catch the rabbit.

Oliver and
the Other Ostriches

A N AUSTERE OSTRICH of awesome authority was
lecturing younger ostriches one day on the superiority
of their species to all other species. "We were known to the
Romans, or, rather, the Romans were known to us," he said.
"They called us *avis struthio*, and we called them Romans.
The Greeks called us *strouthion*, which means 'truthful one,'
or, if it doesn't, it should. We are the biggest birds, and therefore the best."

All his listeners cried, "Hear! Hear!" except a thoughtful
one named Oliver. "We can't fly backward like the hummingbird," he said aloud.

"The hummingbird is losing ground," said the old ostrich. "We are going places, we are moving forward."

"Hear! Hear!" cried all the other ostriches except Oliver.

"We lay the biggest eggs and therefore the best eggs,"
continued the old lecturer.

"The robin's eggs are prettier," said Oliver.

"Robins' eggs produce nothing but robins," said the old
ostrich. "Robins are lawn-bound worm addicts."

"Hear! Hear!" cried all the other ostriches except Oliver.

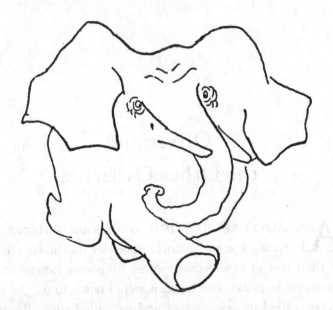

"We get along on four toes, whereas Man needs ten," the elderly instructor reminded his class.

"But Man can fly sitting down, and we can't fly at all," commented Oliver.

The old ostrich glared at him severely, first with one eye and then the other. "Man is flying too fast for a world that is round," he said. "Soon he will catch up with himself, in a great rear-end collision, and Man will never know that what hit Man from behind was Man."

"Hear! Hear!" cried all the other ostriches except Oliver.

"We can make ourselves invisible in time of peril by sticking our heads in the sand," ranted the lecturer. "Nobody else can do that."

"How do we know we can't be seen if we can't see?" demanded Oliver.

"Sophistry!" cried the old ostrich, and all the other ostriches except Oliver cried, "Sophistry!" not knowing what it meant.

Just then the master and the class heard a strange alarming sound, a sound like thunder growing close and growing closer. It was not the thunder of weather, though, but the thunder of a vast herd of rogue elephants in full stampede, frightened by nothing, fleeing nowhere. The old ostrich and all the other ostriches except Oliver quickly stuck their heads in the sand. Oliver took refuge behind a large nearby rock until the storm of beasts had passed, and when he came out he beheld a sea of sand and bones and feathers—all that was left of the old teacher and his disciples. Just to be sure, however, Oliver called the roll, but there was no answer until he came to his own name. "Oliver," he said.

"Here! Here!" said Oliver, and that was the only sound there was on the desert except for a faint, final rumble of thunder on the horizon.

MORAL: *Thou shalt not build thy house,*
nor yet thy faith, upon the sand.

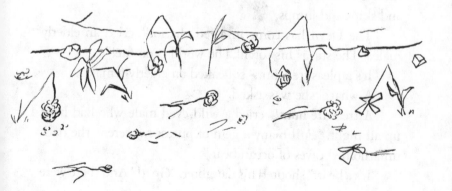

The Shore
and the Sea

A SINGLE EXCITED lemming started the exodus, crying, "Fire!" and running toward the sea. He may have
seen the sunrise through the trees, or waked from a fiery
nightmare, or struck his head against a stone, producing
stars. Whatever it was, he ran and ran, and as he ran he was
joined by others, a mother lemming and her young, a night-
watchlemming on his way home to bed, and assorted revelers
and early risers.

"The world is coming to an end!" they shouted, and as
the hurrying hundreds turned into thousands, the reasons for
their headlong flight increased by leaps and bounds and hops
and skips and jumps.

"The Devil has come in a red chariot!" cried an elderly
male. "The sun is his torch! The world is on fire!"

"It's a pleasure jaunt," squeaked an elderly female.

"A what?" she was asked.

"A treasure hunt!" cried a wild-eyed male who had been
up all night. "Full many a gem of purest ray serene the dark
unfathomed caves of ocean bear."

"It's a bear!" shouted his daughter. "Go it!" And there were those among the fleeing thousands who shouted "Goats!" and "Ghosts!" until there were almost as many different alarms as there were fugitives.

One male lemming who had lived alone for many years refused to be drawn into the stampede that swept past his cave like a flood. He saw no flames in the forest, and no devil, or bear, or goat, or ghost. He had long ago decided, since he was a serious scholar, that the caves of ocean bear no gems, but only soggy glub and great gobs of mucky gump. And so he watched the other lemmings leap into the sea and disappear beneath the waves, some crying "We are saved!" and some crying "We are lost!" The scholarly lemming shook his head sorrowfully, tore up what he had written through the years about his species, and started his studies all over again.

MORAL: *All men should strive to learn before they die what they are running from, and to, and why.*

Uncollected Fables

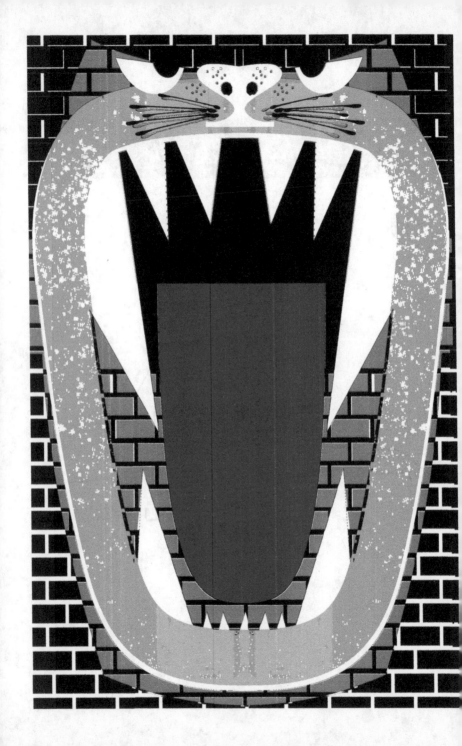

The Flaw in
the Plan

Illustrated by Laurie Rosenwald

T HE CHEETAH NOMINATED himself to lead the Uprising of the Animals, because he was the fastest of them all. "We are going to overthrow America first," the cheetah explained, "and Americans admire speed and stand in fear and awe of it. With all due respect to Leo," he went on, bowing to the lion, "MGM and Androcles have made him a little silly. As for Rhino," he added, bowing to the rhinoceros, "everyone knows that a movie actress not long ago took a snapshot of him in the African jungle and nothing happened."

"I should like to place myself in nomination," said the monkey. "After all, Man sprang from me, and I am not afraid to spring at him. Furthermore, the Uprising was my idea."

"To Man you are a comic," said the cheetah, "who drinks milk from a bottle while riding a tricycle. You are associated with monkey business, shines, and doodle. The elephant will attack first," continued the cheetah, who considered himself elected, "knocking down doors, upsetting buses, breaking the center of Man's line, and then we fleet-footed cats will follow, myself, and the tiger, and the black panther, and the jaguar, and the mountain lion, and the leopard."

"I could divert the attention of the enemy," said the seal, "by balancing my billiard cue and playing 'Three Blind Mice' on my auto horns."

"America's attention is always diverted by something," said the cheetah, "usually by the nervous suspicion that the greatest threat to America is America. Fortunately, at the moment, the enemy is interested in three absorbing things: the latest international romance, the latest Mathilda Madison movie, *The Naked and the Scantily Clad*, and the latest confession recantation, 'I Lied When I Said I Lied When I Said I Lied.'"

"It's easy to beat the Americans on paper," put in the monkey, "but nobody has ever beaten them on anything else."

"Listen," said the cheetah, who hadn't been listening, "and I will brief each of you on the part he must play. We will leave the slow moving animals out of this, the turtle, the porcupine, and the skunk. Then—"

"Point of order, point of order," objected the skunk, and he kept on objecting, but nobody listened.

And so the animals made their plans to overthrow the rule of Man, beginning with a concerted attack on New York. The fleet-footed, quick-minded cheetah rehearsed everybody in the strategy and tactics of the Great Assault. A vote was taken to see if everybody agreed on the plan of campaign, knew what he was supposed to do, and was ready to die for dear old Jungle. All the animals finally voted in favor of the Uprising and the way it had been planned, except the

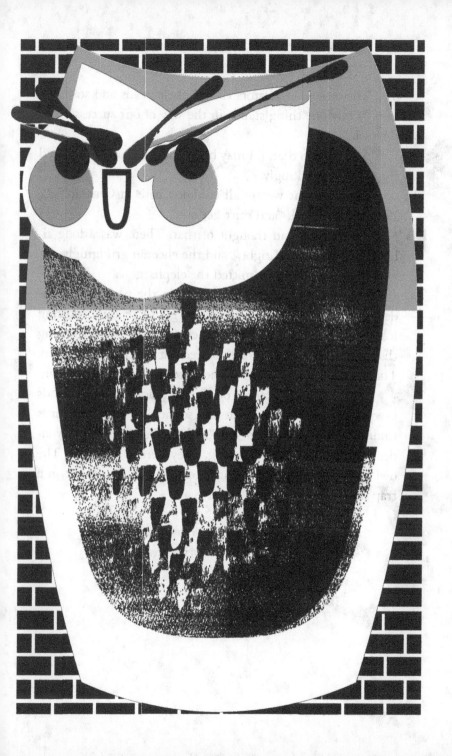

owl. The other conspirators turned their heads and stared at him. "Only one thing stands in the way of our success," said the owl.

"And what is that, if I may be so bold as to ask?" inquired the cheetah mockingly.

"The fact that we are all confined here in Central Park Zoo," said the owl, "and can't get out."

Nobody else had thought of that. There was a long silence. "It's a catch all right," said the cheetah grudgingly.

"It's a drawback," admitted the elephant.

"It places a considerable obstacle in the path of our undertaking," agreed the monkey. "I'm glad I thought to bring it to your attention." Before long everybody began believing that he was the one who had pointed out the flaw in the plan. The cheetah crawled back farther into his cell and lay down.

When the night keeper of the zoo made his final rounds everybody was locked up safe and sound as usual. "Here it is midnight," he said to himself, "and they're all awake. I wonder why." The keeper was wrong. They weren't all awake. The owl was fast asleep, dreaming of catching mice caught in a trap in a cell in a jail.

MORAL: *Stone walls a pretty good prison*
make and iron bars a cage.

A Farewell
to Mandibles

Illustrated by Seymour Chwast

O NE MORNING AN old cockroach who lived in an old bureau in the attic of an old house woke up and felt different, as if something new had been added or something old had been taken away. Both changes, in fact, had occurred. He discovered to his dismay that his mandibles were gone, and he saw two tiny hands in front of him. They held a tiny necktie and they began to put it about his neck and tie it. Then he realized that he was standing before the old, dusty, cracked mirror of the old bureau, and as the hands knotted the tie and pulled it into place, he perceived that he was no longer a cockroach, but a miniature human being.

"God have mercy on me," he said, and he wondered what he meant by that, for he was still part bug. The bug in him cried to be released from the horror of humanization, but the man in him whispered of the fortune he could make on television. The bug in him didn't know what television was, but the man in him hastily explained, and upped the probable size of the fortune he could make. The man in him told hurriedly of the booms, bonanzas, and blessings of manhood, but the bug in him cried, "No, no," at the mention of each of them, wife, children, work, wine, and all the rest, up to and including the sweetness and dignity of dying for Patria, or Patricia, or somebody, and all the eternal life, which is the unique privilege of the human being.

"No, no, no, no, no," cried the tiny manbug, and, just then, he realized his metamorphosis was almost complete, so he ran across the bureau top, threw himself off the edge, fell to the floor, and was instantly killed.

MORAL: *There are worse things than dying.*

Many Pigeons

Illustrated by Victoria Chess

A BANDED HOMING PIGEON whose outfit was the Signal Corps had often observed a charming dovecote in the steeple of an old church, while flying his missions. He dreamed of settling down in the dovecote when all the wars were ended and all the guns were cold. When he realized this wasn't going to happen during his lifetime, he decided to go WOLO, which means We Only Live Once, in Pigeon English. And so he came in for a landing on the threshold of the dovecote. Each pigeon living there figured out who he was while he was still a hundred yards away.

"It's Larkinvar, come out of the Nest!" cried Morna Dove.

"It's Lindbird!" cried her mother.

"Nuts and gargoyles!" growled her father. "He's a stool pigeon."

"He's wearing one handcuff," pointed out a male fantail.

"He's broken away from the cops."

Ed. Note: Thurber wrote three versions of this fable.

"I think he's a jailbird, escaped from the penitentiary," said the fantail's brother. "He has a serial number." For the army pigeon was now so close that all the dovecoters could see his number clearly on the band about one leg.

"He's a passenger pigeon," said a ground dove, who had not been around much but had read a great deal.

"Then he's extinct, or hiding," said the ground dove's uncle, who had not read anything but had been around a great deal.

"He's a fellow passenger pigeon, and they're the worst of all," piped up a cocky young male bird, who hung around cornices. And so only the females, who had mistaken the newcomer for Larkinvar and Lindbird, welcomed him. The others pushed him off the threshold, before he could take off his hat, or catch his breath, or tell his name. Number 137,968, homing pigeon, attached to the United States Signal Corps, turned his back sorrowfully upon his dreamcote and went back to work for the Department of the Army.

MORAL: *There comes an end of toil and fun, but idle guesswork's never done. Or: This, alas, is sadly so; folks would rather believe than know.*

The Ordeal
of No. 137,968

Illustrated by Victoria Roberts

A BANDED HOMING PIGEON whose outfit was the
U.S. Signal Corps, and whose serial number was
137,968, had often observed a charming dovecote while flying a mission or returning from one. He decided to settle
in the dovecote when all the wars were ended and all the
guns were cold, but as time went on he realized that he
was in the service for the duration of his life. So he decided
to go AWOL, or, as he called it, WOLO (We Only Live
Once) and spend the rest of his days among the cute female
turtledoves, mourning doves, ground doves, and others he
had caught sight of on his official trips. The ladies took to
him at once and made him more than welcome. There was
a great flutter and flurry as they tried to guess who he was,
and there was so much conjecture and speculation that he
didn't have a chance to identify himself.

"He's Larkinvar," said Melba Mourning, "or Admiral
Bird."

"Nuts and popcorn," said her mate skeptically. "He's wearing one handcuff. Clearly, he has broken away from the law."

The other males fell in with this theory. "He's a fugitive from a chain gang," said one.

"He killed Cock Robin," cried another.

"He shot the albatross," screamed a third.

But the ladies paid no attention to these dark accusations and went on with their own wishing and wondering.

"He's a war bird," piped up Lorna Turtle. "I love him for the dangers he has known."

"He's Lindbird," tweeted Greta Ground. "He's the great flyer that discovered France."

During all this fuss and feathers, Number 137,968 was not able to get in a word.

"Why doesn't he say something?" asked a suspicious male fantail.

"All is not gold that is silent, you know. He is plainly a fake."

"He's a passenger pigeon," shouted George Mourning.

"Passenger pigeons are extinct," his mate reminded him.

"You're not extinct unless something was the matter," said George darkly.

"If he's not a passenger, he's a fellow passenger, and that's worse,"

cried a common young street pigeon. "I say unfeather and tar him!" And, in spite of the tears and pleadings of the lady doves, the males unfeathered and tarred the newcomer and pushed him out of the dovecote, and watched him flutter to the ground like a shoe.

Number 137,968 had to walk all the way back to his Signal Corps unit, which took him forty-three days. Nobody believed his story of where he had been and what had happened. "He's been living in sin," said the wife of Captain Pigeon. "He got stiff and fell in a tar wagon," decided Major Pigeon. "He got the worst of it in a street fight with common sparrows," cried the wife of Colonel Pigeon. And so Number 137,968 was court-martialed and discharged from the service on a total of nineteen or twenty different counts involving hypothetical misconduct in ten or fifteen places, unnamed and unknown.

MORAL: *There comes an end of toil and fun,*
but human guesswork's never done.

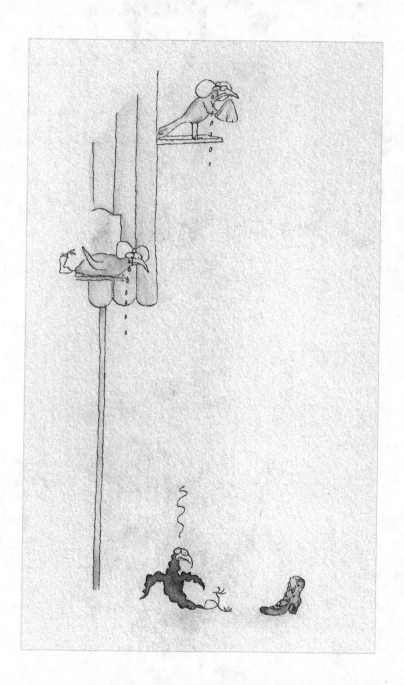

The Pigeon Who
Wouldn't Go Home

Illustrated by Victoria Roberts

A HOMING PIGEON, returning from a mission, flew closer than he ever had before to a belfry that had fascinated him on previous trips. It was the belfry of an old abandoned church and it was full of attractive female fantails and, of course, many proud, pompous, parading, preening, pirouetting, possessive males. The closer the homing pigeon flew to the fascinating belfry and its dovecote of desirable cuties, the more [fascinated? fearless?] he became. He decided all of a sudden, catching a captivating close-up of a flirtatious fantail, to [abandon? desert? quit?] the army Signal Corps—for he was a banded grommet flyer—and live in the belfry.

Everything went well for about nine seconds. The females liked the debonair newcomer, but the males hated the sinister intruder.

Ed. Note: In this recasting of the story, a few handwritten words remain uncertain; they are designated with likely guesses in brackets.

"He has a slave bracelet on his leg. Isn't that sweet?" said a female.

"It's a handcuff," said her mate.

"He's a jailbird. With a serial number," said another male.

"He has a police record as long as your leg."

By nightfall gossip and guesswork had made the new arrival a stool pigeon, an infiltrator, a decoy, a bird of prey, and a lark in dove's feathers. Meantime the gentleman caller was having a wonderful time billing and cooing with the gals. "He's a seducer," said one of the males.

"A bigamist," said another.

"A sex maniac," said a third.

"Wanted for murder," said a fourth.

"And robbery," said a fifth. "That bracelet he wears has what was stolen."

And so the accusations mounted. "He killed Cock Robin."

"He shot an albatross."

"He's wanted for the Sunday Pigeon Murders."

At this a wiser old carrier pigeon who had once worked for the post office woke up in a corner of the belfry. "He is a member in good flying of the U.S. Signal Corps," he said. "The leg band is his credential."

But a fiery young pigeon broke in crying, "He's a passenger pigeon, a fellow traveler."

"He can't truly be a fellow traveler if he hasn't any feathers," said the wise old carrier, but they didn't know what he meant and didn't care. Under the leadership of the fiery young pigeon, the others set upon the sinister intruder, injuring one of his eyes, pulling out most of his feathers, spraining one of his wings, and dragging him from the belfry.

"Tar and unfeather the rascal!" cried the fiery young pigeon as they tarred and unfeathered him.

As the result of his [misjudgment? misconduct?] he was grounded for three weeks when he finally dragged himself back to his post.

MORAL: *Neighbor, stranger, friend, or foe, the world would rather believe than know.*

The Possum Who
Wasn't Playing Dead

Illustrated by Mark Ulriksen

TWO POSSUMS, A female and her mate, quarreled one night so long and late that Inspector Mastiff and Sergeant Dachshund came out to investigate. They found the female possum smoothing her hair with an automatic, and putting a record on the gramophone. "My mate is playing like he was dead," she said coolly.

"He's playing plenty good like he was dead, because he is," said Mastiff, bending over the body behind the sofa.

"If I could shoot like I used to could, I could of done it, but I can't, and so I didn't," explained the possum's widow.

Sergeant Dachshund was writing in his notebook: "These kind of murders are getting more all the time. It's got so a male can't get up for a drink in the night without his mate shoots him down before he can climb back in bed."

Inspector Mastiff stepped quietly to the gramophone and turned off "Love is a Many-Splendored Thing." He searched the record albums hastily, until he came upon "Kentucky Babe," and he put it on the gramophone. The female possum

was twenty feet away when the soloist came to "Possum for your breakfast, when your sleepin' time is done," but she shot the record off the turntable with the ease of an expert.

"You can still shoot as good as you used to could," growled Inspector Mastiff.

"And that's enough evidence for he and I," piped up Sergeant Dachshund.

"Whatta you gudda do?" quavered the guilty possum.

"We gudda play house—station house," grunted Inspector Mastiff, and he and the sergeant led her to their squad car.

"Okay, I done it," said the late possum's widow on the way to the police station. "He come home once too often with bunny hairs on his lapel. You don't get them hairs at no rat race, like where he always said he was."

As the car sped along, Sergeant Dachshund thought ruefully, "Everybody who wants to die with their boots on should go to bed fully clothed."

MORAL: *Husbandslaughter is occasionally just, but why should the mother tongue bite the dust?*

The Starling
and the Crow

Illustrated by Eric Hanson

A STARLING, one of a thousand that lived and bickered in a great elm, met a crow one morning and passed the time of day. They met frequently after that, since their daily paths crossed, as the crow flew to the cornfield and the starling to the rye. They didn't say much, for the starling spoke only a little crow and the crow's starling was far from fluent. But the word got around among the starlings that the familiarity of the starling and the crow was not good.

"He's selling us out to the crows," cried an important starling who had started the story that starlings were starlings because they owned the stars. "He has given them the plans of our nests, he believes in their caws, his father was a crow on his mother's side."

242

The innocent starling demanded a public hearing, but the starlings made so much noise accusing him, and one another, of unstarling activities and pro-crowism, that he couldn't make himself heard.

"Are you a crow or aren't you?" shouted Senator Upstarling.

The starling said, "No, I am not," but he couldn't be heard above the babble and bickering, threats, warnings, accusations, innuendoes, and the shouts of the photographers and newspapermen.

"Guilty of whatever it is he's guilty of," declared the judge. "I can't hear a goddamn thing and I'm late for a date with fly-catcher in the rye."

"Throw him to the butcher birds!" cried half of the star-lings, and there was a great pecking and clawing and flying of feathers, during which the crows attacked the elm and took it over without any trouble to speak of.

MORAL: *Familiarity also breeds contempt proceedings.*

The Generalissimo of All
the Field Mice in the World

Illustrated by Edel Rodriguez

T HE GENERALISSIMO OF all the Field Mice in the World lived in a wild, secluded Nebraska field, which the Generalissimo believed was all the earth and the universe. If you burrow too far in any direction, he decreed, you will burrow your way out of the planet and plunge into everlasting space. "What happens to you then?" his wife asked him one night, after removing his army boots and his scarlet and gray uniform. "There is no Finality," said the Generalissimo, with finality. "You just keep on falling forever."

All the other creatures that lived below the grass were in awe of the great field mouse who knew so much about everything. "I am a general and a philosopher," he would say, drinking a liquor made of dandelion roots and oil of viper's bugloss. "A general is no good unless he can justify his actions, and a philosopher is no good unless he can protect his inactivity by throwing a military guard around his seclusion." The other field mice and the moles and chipmunks and gophers didn't know what the

Generalissimo was talking about, but they figured that if it was beyond their comprehension it might be worth believing in. They came to hate creatures like the crickets and grasshoppers, who were just as smart as their leaders.

For a time the Generalissimo was satisfied with the title he had forced the field mice to confer on him by acclamation, but then he decided that they wanted him to be the Generalissimore, and, in the end, the Generalissimost. As soon as he had been given this magnificent title, it became clear to him that the other creatures who lived underground needed to be protected from their own freedom. He called in his Chief Burrower and explained that his burrows must be connected up with the burrows of the moles, the chipmunks, and the gophers. When the Chief Burrower explained that this would be aggression he disappeared one night and was never seen again, and a new Chief Burrower took his place. "Aggression," said the Generalissimost, "is anything that stands in the way of our protecting the other creatures from their freedom." So the field mice began to extend their tunnels and corridors until they were all connected up with the tunnels and corridors of the neighboring moles, chipmunks, and gophers.

_____

Ed. Note: This is an unfinished fable. The manuscript ends here.

The Bright Emperor

Illustrated by R. O. Blechman

T HE PARTICULAR BEETLES whose vast empire was the small backyard of a house on Fifth Avenue were astonished one day in May when one of their members, known as a ne'er-do-well, returned after a long absence wearing a shining silver helmet on his head. Perched just above his

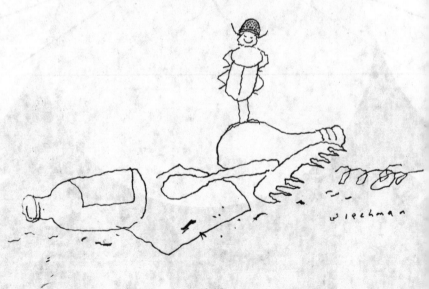

eyes, it allowed his feelers full play, and was very becoming and impressive, although it seemed a trifle heavy for one unused to wearing anything on his head except an occasional drop of rain. The emperor of the beetles, a plain, unadorned beetle, lived in an overturned box that had once belonged to a dog. There was a damp rug in the box. This palace was looked upon by the beetles as the finest palace in the world.

When the emperor heard the uproar that followed the return of the beetle with the silver helmet, he sent for him. Silver Helmet refused to go to the emperor for the simple reason that his helmet was so high he couldn't get inside the box that was the emperor's palace. There was just room for ordinary beetles, without anything on their heads, to crawl into the box. Silver Helmet sent word to the emperor that if the emperor wanted to see him the emperor would have to come outside. This arrogant pronouncement awed the beetles who heard it and when Silver Helmet went on with a long rigmarole about how the helmet had been placed on his head by a goddess—a great and magnificent goddess, who was supremely lovely and benign—they began to believe that the brightly crowned beetle had been divinely ordained to seize the throne from the emperor and rule over them in his stead. Times weren't any worse in the beetle empire than they were anywhere else at this particular epoch, but the beetles gradually talked themselves into believing that the old emperor was responsible for everything that hadn't gone exactly right and that the beetle with the silver crown would bring an unheard-of peace and prosperity to the community. There were a few beetles who took no interest one way or the other, because they believed that the world was coming to an end anyway, but the great majority rallied around the silver-crowned beetle and declared him emperor. The dethroned emperor, warned of the revolt, fled just in time, with his wife and seventy-eight children. They escaped to another kingdom simply by crawling through a small hole in the fence, leading to the next yard. The new emperor took up his headquarters under a smaller box in the yard into which he could crawl, helmet and all, and ruled the beetles, in a rather so-so fashion, for several weeks, sitting around in the sun, taking no part in the gathering of food or in anything else, and elaborating on his story of the beautiful goddess who had given him the silver helmet. He asserted that he was immortal and that he was glorified and that he was immune from illness or injury and that the laws which applied to everybody else did not apply to him. The other beetles were deeply impressed and brought him the nicest bits of cereal and other delicacies that they found. He grew so fat that he could squeeze in and out of his palace only by a great effort and still keep his silver crown on.

One day a lady and a small child who lived in the house to which the yard belonged came out into the yard because it was a fine sunshiny day. The little girl, who was four years old, and known as the nastiest child in the neighborhood, saw the silver-crowned beetle and set up a cry. "Oh, Grace," she cried (for she called her mother Grace), "look, there's the bug I caught and put my thimble on!" She pointed at the emperor's magic crown, which was, indeed, a tiny thimble that had been a birthday present to the little girl from her Aunt Clara, who lives in Bronxville. "Well, of all things," said the child's mother, and she started for the beetle. It ran and so did all the others, but whereas all the others escaped, the emperor was unable to find any hole or crevice large enough for him to get into hurriedly. The child's mother killed him with an old broom, used for sweeping up trash, and recovered the thimble. "Now don't you ever put it on a bug's head again," she said. "The idea! What would Aunt Clara think?"

After the mother and child had gone back into the house, the beetles crept cautiously out of their hiding places and looked, in awe, at the dead emperor. He looked like any dead beetle now. Then they sent a delegate into the next yard to ask the old emperor to return, which he did, with his wife and ninety-eight children, and the beetles all settled down to a drab and uneventful life. Of the many morals which attach to the story, the one I like best is something about never accepting a gift of radiance from a woman, of whatever age, for the moment of glory it gives cannot compensate for the disaster which must inevitably follow.

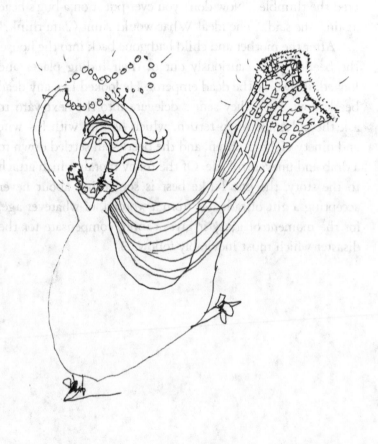

The Princess
and the Tin Box

Illustrated by Blair Thornley

ONCE UPON A TIME, in a far country, there lived a king whose daughter was the prettiest princess in the world. Her eyes were like the cornflower, her hair was sweeter than the hyacinth, and her throat made the swan look dusty.

From the time she was a year old, the princess had been showered with presents. Her nursery looked like Cartier's window. Her toys were all made of gold or platinum or diamonds or emeralds. She was not permitted to have wooden blocks or china dolls or rubber dogs or linen books, because such materials were considered cheap for the daughter of a king.

When she was seven, she was allowed to attend the wedding of her brother and throw real pearls at the bride instead of rice. Only the nightingale, with his lyre of gold, was permitted to sing for the princess. The common blackbird, with his boxwood flute, was kept out of the palace grounds. She walked in silver-and-samite slippers to a sapphire-and-topaz bathroom and slept in an ivory bed inlaid with rubies.

On the day the princess was eighteen, the king sent a royal ambassador to the courts of five neighboring kingdoms to announce that he would give his daughter's hand in marriage to the prince who brought her the gift she liked the most.

The first prince to arrive at the palace rode a swift white stallion and laid at the feet of the princess an enormous apple made of solid gold which he had taken from a dragon who had guarded it for a thousand years. It was placed on a long ebony table set up to hold the gifts of the princess's suitors.

The second prince, who came on a gray charger, brought her a nightingale made of a thousand diamonds, and it was placed beside the golden apple.

The third prince, riding on a black horse, carried a great jewel box made of platinum and sapphires, and it was placed next to the diamond nightingale.

The fourth prince, astride a fiery yellow horse, gave the princess a gigantic heart made of rubies and pierced by an emerald arrow. It was placed next to the platinum-and-sapphire jewel box.

Now the fifth prince was the strongest and handsomest of all the five suitors, but he was the son of a poor king whose realm had been overrun by mice and locusts and wizards and mining engineers so that there was nothing much of value left in it. He came plodding up to the palace of the princess on a plow horse and he brought her a small tin box filled with mica and feldspar and hornblende which he had picked up on the way.

The other princes roared with disdainful laughter when they saw the tawdry gift the fifth prince had brought to the princess. But she examined it with great interest and squealed with delight, for all her life she had never seen tin before or mica or feldspar or hornblende. The tin box was placed next to the ruby heart pierced with an emerald arrow.

"Now," the king said to his daughter, "you must select the gift you like best and marry the prince that brought it."

The princess smiled and walked up to the table and picked up the present she liked the most. It was the platinum-and-sapphire jewel box, the gift of the third prince.

"The way I figure it," she said, "is this. It is a very large and expensive box, and when I am married, I will meet many admirers who will give me precious gems with which to fill it to the top. Therefore, it is the most valuable of all the gifts my suitors have brought me and I like it the best."

The princess married the third prince that very day in the midst of great merriment and high revelry. More than a hundred thousand pearls were thrown at her, and she loved it.

MORAL: *All those who thought the princess was going to select the tin box filled with worthless stones instead of one of the other gifts will kindly stay after class and write one hundred times on the blackboard "I would rather have a hunk of aluminum silicate than a diamond necklace."*

The Last Clock:
A Fable for the Time,
Such as It Is of Man

Illustrated by Calef Brown

I N A C O U N T R Y the other side of tomorrow, an ogre who had eaten a clock and had fallen into the habit of eating clocks was eating a clock in the clockroom of his castle when his ogress and their ilk knocked down the locked door and shook their hairy heads at him.

"Wulsa malla?" gurgled the ogre, for too much clock oil had turned all his "t"s to "l"s.

"Just look at this room!" exclaimed the ogress, and they all looked at the room, the ogre with eyes as fogged as the headlights of an ancient limousine. The stone floor of the room was littered with fragments of dials, oily coils and springs, broken clock hands, and pieces of pendulums. "I've brought a doctor to look at you," the ogress said.

The doctor wore a black beard, carried a black bag, and gave the ogre a black look. "This case is clearly not in my area," he said.

The ogre struck three, and the doctor flushed.

"This is a case for a clockman," the doctor said, "for the problem is not what clocks have done to the ogre but what the ogre has done to clocks."

"Wulsa malla?" the ogre gurgled again.

"Eating clocks has turned all his 't's to 'l's," the ogress said. "That's what clocks have done to him."

"Then your clockman may have to call in consultation a semanticist or a dictionist or an etymologist or a syntaxman," the non-clock doctor said, and he bowed stiffly and left the room.

The next morning, the ogress brought into the clock-room a beardless man with a box of tools under his arm. "I've brought a clockman to see you," she told the ogre.

"No, no, no," said the beardless man with a box of tools under his arm. "I'm not a clockman. I thought you said clog-man. I'm a clogman. I cannot ethically depart from my area, which is clogged drains and gutters. I get mice out of pipes, and bugs out of tubes, and moles out of tiles, and there my area ends." The clogman bowed and went away.

"Wuld wuzzle?" the ogre wanted to know. He hiccuped, and something went spong! "That was an area man, but the wrong area," the ogress explained. "I'll get a general practi-tioner." And she went away and came back with a general practitioner.

"This is a waste of time," he said. "As a general practi-tioner, modern style, I treat only generals. This patient is not even a private. He sounds to me like a public place—a clock tower, perhaps, or a belfry."

"What should I do?" asked the ogress. "Send for a tower man, or a belfry man?"

"I shall not venture an opinion," said the general practitioner. "I am a specialist in generals, one of whom has just lost command of his army and of all his faculties, and doesn't know what time it is. Good day." And the general practitioner went away.

The ogre cracked a small clock, as if it were a large walnut, and began eating it. "Wulsy wul?" the ogre asked.

The ogress, who could now talk clocktalk fluently, even oilily, but wouldn't, left the room to look up specialists in an enormous volume entitled *Who's Who in Areas*. She soon became lost in a list of titles: clockmaker, clocksmith, clockwright, clockmonger, clockician, clockometrist, clockologist, and a hundred others dealing with clockness, clockism, clockship, clockdom, clockation, clockition, and clockhood.

The ogress decided to call on an old inspirationalist who had once advised her father not to worry about a giant he was worrying about. The inspirationalist had said to the ogress's father, "Don't pay any attention to it, and it will go away." And the ogress's father had paid no attention to it, and it had gone away, taking him with it, and this had pleased the ogress. The inspirationalist was now a very old man whose inspirationalism had become a jumble of mumble. "The final experience should not be mummum," he mumbled.

The ogress said, "But what is mummum?"

"Mummum," said the inspirationalist, "is what the final experience should not be." And he mumbled to a couch, lay down upon it, and fell asleep.

As the days went on, the ogre ate all the clocks in the town—mantel clocks, grandfather clocks, traveling clocks, stationary clocks, alarm clocks, eight-day clocks, steeple clocks, and tower clocks—sprinkling them with watches, as if the watches were salt and pepper, until there were no more watches. People overslept, and failed to go to work, or to church, or any-place else where they had to be on time. Factories closed down, shopkeepers shut up their shops, schools did not open, trains no longer ran, and people stayed at home. The town council held an emergency meeting and its members arrived at all hours, and some did not show up at all.

A psychronologist was called to the witness stand to testify as to what should be done. "This would appear to be a clear case of clock-eating, but we should not jump easily to conclusions," he said. "We have no scientific data whatever on clock-eating, and hence no controlled observation. All things, as we know, are impossible in this most impossible of all impossible worlds. That being the case, no such thing as we think has happened could have happened. Thus the situation does not fall within the frame of my discipline. Good day, gentlemen." The psychronologist glanced at where his wristwatch should have been and, not finding it there, was disturbed. "I have less than no time at all," he said, "which means that I am late for my next appointment." And he hurriedly left the council room.

The Lord Mayor of the town, arriving late to preside over the council meeting, called a clockonomist to the stand. "What we have here," said the clockonomist, "appears on the surface to be a clockonomic crisis. It is the direct opposite of what is known, in my field, as a glut of clocks. That is, instead of there being more clocks than the consumer needs, so that the price of clocks would decrease, the consumer has consumed all the clocks. This should send up the cost of clocks sharply, but we are faced with the unique fact that there are no clocks. Now, as a clockonomist, my concern is the economy of clocks, but where there are no clocks there can be no such economy. The area, in short, has disappeared."

"What do you suggest, then?" demanded the Lord Mayor.

"I suggest," said the clockonomist, "that it is now high time I go into some other line of endeavor, or transfer my clockonomy to a town which has clocks. Good day, gentlemen." And the clockonomist left the council room. A clockosopher next took the witness stand. "If it is high time," he said, "then there is still time. The question is: How high is high time? It means, if it means anything, which I doubt, that it is time to act. I am not an actor, gentlemen, but a clockosopher, whose osophy is based upon clocks, not necessarily upon their physical existence, but upon clocks as a concept. We still have clocks as a concept, but this meeting is concerned chiefly with clocks as objects. Thus its deliberations fall well outside my range of interest, and I am simply wasting time here, or would be if there were time to waste. Good day, gentlemen." And the clockosopher left the council room.

The clockmakers of the town, who had been subpoenaed, were then enjoined, in a body, from making more clocks. "You have been supplying the ogre with clocks," the Lord Mayor said severely, "whether intentionally or willy-nilly is irrelevant. You have been working hand in glove, or clock in hand, with the ogre." The clockmakers left, to look for other work.

"I should like to solve this case," the Lord Mayor said, "but, as a container of clocks, he would have to be exported, not deported. Unfortunately, the law is clear on this point: clocks may not be exported in any save regulation containers, and the human body falls outside that legal definition."

Three weeks to the day after the ogre had eaten the last clock, he fell ill and took to his bed, and the ogress sent for the chief diagnostician of the Medical Academy, a diagnostician familiar with so many areas that totality itself had become to him only a part of wholeness. "The trouble is," said the chief diagnostician, "we don't know what the trouble is. Nobody has ever eaten all the clocks before, so it is impossible to tell whether the patient has clockitis, clockosis, clockoma, or clocktheria. We are also faced with the possibility that there may be no such diseases. The patient may have one of the minor clock ailments, if there are any, such as clockets, clockles, clocking cough, ticking pox, or clumps. We shall have to develop area men who will find out about such areas, if such areas exist, which, until we find out that they do, we must assume do not."

"What if he dies?" demanded the ogress eagerly.

"Then," said the chief diagnostician, "we shall bury him." And the chief diagnostician left the ogre's room and the castle.

The case of the town's clocklessness was carried to the Supreme Council, presided over by the Supreme Magistrate. "Who is prosecuting whom?" the Supreme Magistrate demanded. The Supreme Prosecutor stood up. "Let somebody say something, and I will object," he said. "We have to start somewhere, even if we start nowhere."

A housewife took the witness stand. "Without a clock," she said, "I cannot even boil a three-minute egg."

"Objection," said the Supreme Prosecutor. "One does not have to boil a three-minute egg. A three-minute egg, by definition, has already been boiled for three minutes, or it wouldn't be a three-minute egg."

"Objection sustained," droned the Supreme Magistrate.

The Leader of the Opposition then took the stand. "The party in power has caused the mess in the ogre's castle," he said.

"Objection," said the Supreme Prosecutor. "There isn't any party in power. The ogre was the party in power, but he no longer has any power. Furthermore, the mess caused by the party cleaning up the mess caused by the party in power, which is no longer in power, would be worse than the mess left by the party that was in power."

"Objection sustained," droned the Supreme Magistrate.

The Secretary of Status Quo was the next man to take the stand. "We are not getting anywhere," he said, "and therefore we should call a summit conference without agenda. A summit conference without agenda is destined to get even less than nowhere, but its deliberations will impress those who are impressed by deliberations that get less than nowhere. This has unworked in the past, and it will unwork now. If we get less than nowhere fast enough, we shall more than hold our own, for everything is circular and cyclical, and where there are no clocks, clockwise and counterclockwise are the same."

"Objection," said the Supreme Prosecutor. "We are dealing here with a purely internal matter, caused by the consumer's having consumed all the clocks."

"Objection sustained," droned the Supreme Magistrate.

The Man in the Street now took the stand. "Why don't we use sundials?" he demanded.

"I challenge the existence of the witness," said the Supreme Prosecutor. "He says he is the Man in the Street, but he is, in fact, the Man in the Supreme Council Room. Furthermore, sundials work only when the sun is shining, and nobody cares what time it is when the sun is shining."

The Man in the Street left the witness chair, and nobody noticed his going, since the Supreme Prosecutor had established the fact that he had not been there. There was a long silence in the Supreme Council Room, a silence so deep one could have heard a pin drop, if a pin had been dropped, but nobody dropped a pin. What everybody in the council room heard, in the long, deep silence, was the slow tick-tock of a clock, a wall clock, the clock on the wall behind the Supreme Magistrate's bench. The officials and the witnesses and the spectators had grown so used to not hearing clocks it wasn't until the clock struck the hour that they realized there was a wall clock on the wall.

The Supreme Magistrate was the first to speak. "Unless I am mightily mistaken, and I usually am, we have here the solution to all our problems," he said, "namely, a clock. Unless there is an objection and I sustain the objection, which I do not think I shall, we will place this clock in the clock tower of the town, where it can be seen by one and all. Then we shall once again know what time it is. The situation will be cleared up, and the case dismissed."

"One minute," said the Supreme Prosecutor, and everybody waited a minute until he spoke again. "What is to prevent the ogre from eating the clock in the clock tower?"

"If you are asking me," said the Supreme Magistrate, "I do not know, but I do not have to confess my ignorance, since affirmations of this sort do not fall within my jurisdiction."

A bailiff stepped to the bench and handed the Supreme Magistrate a folded note. The Magistrate glanced at it, took off his glasses, and addressed all those present. "The ogre is dead," he announced.

"Objection," said the Supreme Prosecutor.

"Objection overruled," said the Magistrate, "if you are objecting to the fact of the ogre's death."

"I accept the ogre's death as a fact," said the Prosecutor, "but we are moving too fast, and I should like to call a specialist to the stand." And he called a specialist to the stand.

"I am a collector," said the specialist. "The clock on the wall is the only clock there is. This makes it not, in fact, a clock but a collector's item, or museum piece. As such, it must be placed in the town museum. One does not spend the coins in a museum. The wineglasses in a museum do not hold wine. The suits of armor in a museum do not contain knights. The clocks in a museum do not tell time. This clock, the last clock there is, must therefore be allowed to run down, and then placed in the museum with proper ceremonies, addresses, and the like."

"I move that this be done," the Prosecutor said.

"I should like to continue to know, as much as everybody else, what time it is," pronounced the Supreme Magistrate. "Under the circumstances, however, there is but one thing I can do in conformity with the rule which establishes the inalienable fact that the last clock is a collector's item, or museum piece. I therefore decree that the last clock, the clock here on the wall, be allowed to run down, and then placed in the town museum, with proper ceremonies, addresses, and the like."

The next day, at nine minutes of twelve o'clock noon, the last clock ran down and stopped. It was then placed in the town museum as a collector's item, or museum piece, with proper ceremonies, addresses, and the like. Among those who spoke were the Lord Mayor, the Secretary of

Status Quo, and the Supreme Magistrate. They all chose the same subjects, without verbs or predicates, and the subjects were these: glorious past, unlimited opportunity, challenging futures, dedication, inspired leadership, enlightened followership, rededication, moral fiber, spiritual values, outer space, inner man, higher ideals, lower taxes, unflagging enthusiasm, unswerving devotion, coordinated efforts, dedicated rededication, and rededicated dedication.

After that, nobody in town ever knew what time is was. Factories and schools remained closed, church bells no longer rang because the bell ringers no longer knew when to ring them, and dates and engagements were no longer made because nobody knew when to keep them. Trains no longer ran, so nobody left town and no strangers arrived in town to tell the people what time it was. Eventually, the sands of a nearby desert moved slowly and inexorably toward the timeless town, and in the end it was buried.

Eras, epochs, and eons passed before a party of explorers from another planet began digging in the sands above the buried town. They were descendants of people from Earth who had reached Venus a thousand years before and intermarried with Venusians. Among them were a young man and a young woman, and it was their fortune to be the first to come upon the ancient library of the old inspirationalist. Among some papers still preserved upon his desk were the last things he had written—bits of poetry from the grand Old Masters and the minor poets. One of these fragments read, "How goes the night, boy? The moomoon is down. I have not heard the clock." And the very last words his wavery pen had put on paper:

We can make our lives sublime,
And, departing, leave behind us,
Mummum in the sands of time.

"What is mummum?" the young woman asked.

"I don't know," the young man said, "but something tells me we shall find a lot of it." They went on digging, and, in the end, came upon the last clock in the town museum, so clogged with sand they could not tell what it had once been used for, and so they marked it "Antique mechanism. Function uncertain. Possibly known to ancients as mummum." And they took it back to Venus, in a cargo rocket ship, with other mysterious relics of the Time of Man on Earth.

January 12, 1959*

Bill, old fellow:

Take this one up tenderly, for it's my heart. I worry a little bit, foolishly perhaps, because of my fear that some of your dedicated editors may not so much read this as process it. I have processed it myself, screened it, and rewritten it five times from start to finish. I don't have to tell you, a musician, that the repetitions, a word that is anathema to *The New Yorker* boys and girls, are not only intentional, but have been worked out with exceeding care. I won't bother your staff by pointing out the indirect influences of Browning's triple rhyme scheme (though I use no actual rhymes), and what Leonard Bernstein might call the architecture of the andante cantabile. The boys and girls will understand this, but someone is sure to point out the use of "so clogged" and "and so" in one sentence. Tell them the hell with it. Some keen mind may even suggest variance for "took the stand" and "took the witness chair." Tell them to forget it. If anybody says this is uncharacteristic and familiar, I shall kill him.

---

*   This letter from Thurber accompanied his submission of "The Last Clock" manuscript to *The New Yorker* editor William Shawn.

The immediate inspiration occurred to me when I was dozing during the fourth quarter of the last Giants-Browns football game, when the announcer said, "With only 35 seconds left to go, all the Giants have to do is eat up the clock." For further implementation on such phenomena the kids might read *The Dynamics of Insight* by Alexander Reid Martin, or, better yet, not read it. There is nothing in this piece I am unaware of and, for Jesus sake, don't let any of the keen minds point out that there is illogic in the statements of some of the specialists. I don't have to tell you that this is a moving study, moving and a little frightening, too, of what modern mummum has done, and is doing, to muxx up the condition of man. Incidentally, *The New Yorker* review of "The Human Condition" should easily win the Pulitzer Prize for dullness.

Affectionately,
J. T.

About the Author

THE TWENTIETH CENTURY'S most popular American humorist, James Thurber (1894–1961) authored nearly two dozen collections of drawings, essays, stories, fables, and biographical works—much of which he published as a founding voice of *The New Yorker* magazine. Along with a shelf of classic children's books, a gem-like autobiography, *My Life and Hard Times*, and two Broadway productions, Thurber created spontaneous, unstudied drawings that profoundly changed the character of cartooning and expanded the very possibilities of an illustrated line.

About the Author

About the Editor

M ICHAEL J. ROSEN has published five volumes of
James Thurber's uncollected or unpublished work,
including the 2019 monograph, *A Mile and a Half of Lines:
The Art of James Thurber* (Ohio State University Press), that co-
incides with the first major exhibition of Thurber's artwork at
the Columbus Museum of Art. From 1982 to 2001, he served
as literary director of The Thurber House, a center for readers
and writers in the restored boyhood home of James Thurber
in Columbus, Ohio. During that time, Rosen helped to create The Thurber Prize for American Humor and a biennial
anthology of contemporary humor. Like Thurber, he is a
native son of Columbus, Ohio, a writer of children's books, an
illustrator, humorist, and a consummate dog person.

ALSO BY JAMES THURBER

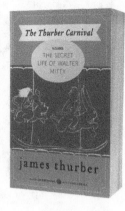

THE THURBER CARNIVAL
Available in Paperback

The Thurber Carnival is the author's personal culling of his best short stories, tributes, fantasies, parodies, and commentary from his first eight books—much of which first appeared in the pages of *The New Yorker*. It features the autobiographical stories of *My Life and Hard Times*, and as well several folios of his inimitable and timeless cartoons. An instant bestseller and Thurber's most acclaimed volume, *The Thurber Carnival* has been continuously in print since 1945.

IS SEX NECESSARY?
OR WHY YOU FEEL THE WAY YOU DO
Available in Paperback

The first book of prose published by either James Thurber or E. B. White, *Is Sex Necessary?* combines the humor and genius of both authors to examine those great mysteries of life—romance, love, and marriage.

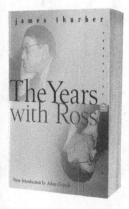

THE YEARS WITH ROSS
Available in Paperback

At the helm of *The New Yorker*, America's most influential literary magazine, for more than half a century, Harold Ross introduced the country to a host of exciting talent. But no one could have written about this irascible, eccentric genius more affectionately or more critically than James Thurber, whose portrait of Ross captures not only a complex literary giant but a historic friendship and a glorious era as well.

HarperCollins*Publishers*
DISCOVER GREAT AUTHORS, EXCLUSIVE OFFERS, AND MORE AT HC.COM.

ALSO BY JAMES THURBER

MY LIFE AND HARD TIMES
Available in Paperback

James Thurber looks back at his own life growing up in
Columbus, Ohio, with the same humor and sharp wit
that defined his famous sketches and writings.

THE JAMES THURBER
AUDIO COLLECTION:
FABLES AND SELECTED STORIES
BY JAMES THURBER
Available in Audio

Collected fables and short stories from literary legend
James Thurber, Performed by Keith Olbermann.

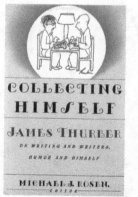

COLLECTING HIMSELF:
JAMES THURBER ON WRITING AND
WRITERS, HUMOR AND HIMSELF
Available in eBook

Collecting Himself is a one-of-a-kind compilation of
James Thurber's vintage writings, featuring previously
unanthologized articles, essays, interviews, reviews,
cartoons, parodies, as well as Thurber's reflections on
his work in theater and at *The New Yorker*. An eclectic
body of work that offers a glimpse into Thurber the
man, the philosopher, and the critic.

HarperCollins*Publishers*
DISCOVER GREAT AUTHORS, EXCLUSIVE OFFERS, AND MORE AT HC.COM.